MW01590812

The Teacher

A Novel
Based on a True Story

By
Roger Quam

Copyright © 2013 by Roger Quam

The Teacher
by Roger Quam

Printed in the United States of America

ISBN 9781625096043

All rights reserved solely by the author. The author guarantees all contents are original and do not infringe upon the legal rights of any other person or work. No part of this book may be reproduced in any form without the permission of the author. The views expressed in this book are not necessarily those of the publisher.

Unless otherwise indicated, Bible quotations are taken from the New King James Version. Copyright © 1982 by Thomas Nelson, Inc. Used by permission.

www.xulonpress.com

**Dedicated to my mother, Louise Jenny (Larson) Quam,
who was seven years old and in the country school when
her teacher was shot.**

Chapter 1

March 5, 1913

*T*he morning was cold and windy. It had snowed the previous night. The day was the 5ᵗʰ of March, 1913—a Wednesday. All sixteen children were on their way from their farms to the one-room country schoolhouse in the western Clay County township of Spring Prairie, Minnesota. The teacher, Miss Carrie Wilson, climbed into the sleigh to travel the two miles from the Lewis and Jennie Larson farm where she stayed in a small upstairs bedroom. Along with her in the sleigh were four of the Larson children: Roy, Joe, Freddie, and little Louise. Their father would handle the reins. All five passengers sat in the sleigh patiently waiting for their driver. The horse, Nelly, was accustomed to this short trip to the school, having traveled it many times in the past two years since she was acquired—traded for a pregnant sow in the middle of the winter of 1911.

Frequently, Lewis was unable to make the trip and son Freddie would take the reins. On those days, Nelly would stay in the horse barn during school hours, which was shared with the Zion Lutheran Church across the road from the township school. The barn was able to accommodate several horses and carriages, and had a good supply of feed for them. A spring well was close by to provide fresh water for the school and the church, as well as for the horses.

All the riders in the sleigh had been well fed by Mrs. Jennie Larson at breakfast. The smell of fresh eggs frying in butter, fried ham, and hot muffins had quickly permeated the house and awakened everyone. The muffin recipe had been brought from Sweden in the 1880s and handed down from Jennie's mother. The ham had been kept frozen over winter and now was stored in the pantry ice box.

Lewis looked out the kitchen window at the young woman and the children in the sleigh, and commented in English to Jennie, his Swedish wife, "Carrie is one beautiful woman who doesn't seem to have a steady boyfriend. Why do you suppose that is? At least, no one has come courting her."

Jennie looked out the same window and replied, "Just give her time; she has interested men all over the township and county. Two of our sons are among them, you know."

"Oh, really?" replied Lewis.

"You haven't noticed?" Jennie questioned.

"No, I have not."

"Tell me then, Lewis, have you noticed how two of our sons have taken an interest in dressing up in nice clothes lately and how they are cleaned up when they come to the dinner table at night?"

"I guess you may be right," Lewis answered with a chuckle.

"I know I'm right," Jennie replied. "I know my boys."

"Well," replied Lewis, "as far as I know, no man has come to court her." He put on his hat and gave his wife a peck on the cheek as he walked out the door to his waiting passengers.

The winter had been unusually mild with not much snow. Had it not snowed the night before, the trip to the school would have been made using the family buggy. Both the sleigh and buggy were enclosed enough to shield the riders from the cold and wind, thus lessening the wind chill effects from the cold south wind. Little Louise Larson had tied bells on the inside of both the buggy and the family sleigh at Christmas. Her family abided by her wishes when she insisted on leaving the bells on after the holidays. She was excited about having a birthday in a little over a month when she would be eight years old.

Carrie Wilson seemed a little nervous this particular morning. She had received a letter two days previous that was weighing heavily on her mind. She had slept very little from worrying about it, and her lack of sleep was causing her to doze off to the rhythm of Nelly's hooves striking the frozen roadway through the light, blowing snow. The clicking of the horse's hooves provided an almost musical accompaniment to the bells.

The words in the letter were very disturbing to Miss Carrie, and she had no idea of their full meaning or how to handle it. It was from an old acquaintance from her home back east, in Massachusetts. She had met him the summer before she entered college. After a short dating period she had broken up with him, but he still pursued her with letters. Even more troubling than the letters, he would follow up with an unannounced visit to where she was teaching at the time. It happened once before in Pennsylvania and once in Ohio. The people she was staying with had always promised to protect her. Now the old boyfriend had somehow obtained her current address in Spring Prairie. This particular morning she felt a sense of imminent danger.

Carrie was a tall and beautiful woman of twenty-four years. Many young men had pursued her in the past, both in her college years and in her places of teaching. She had received many marriage proposals from some fine—and some not-so-fine— young gentlemen, some older men, and even some of the older boys who were her students. At this point in her life, she was still dedicated to teaching children to read, write, and understand math. She was in no hurry to settle down, and her one brief foray into romance had turned her off completely on romantic relationships.

Along with teaching the children at the Spring Prairie country school, she also held English classes at the Zion Lutheran Church across the road from the school on Saturday afternoons. Attending this class were some of the parents, grandparents, uncles, and aunts of the schoolchildren. They were struggling with the English language that the children quickly mastered. Carrie figured that she couldn't do a sufficient job with the children unless she could also communicate with their parents. Of greater importance was the ability of the parents to understand what their children were saying in English. Carrie knew that it was important to the families that they be able to function in an English-speaking country while preserving their native languages and heritages.

Two heavy quilts kept the children warm in the rear seat as the covered horse-drawn sleigh drove into the cold wind, making its way toward the country school. Miss Carrie, Lewis, and Freddie wore heavy winter overcoats in the front seat.

The teacher thought about what was planned for her students that morning. There would be the Pledge of Allegiance, the daily Scripture reading and prayer, the weekly spelldown, the American history lesson, reading assignments, and penmanship, all before lunch. She expected the morning to go smoothly. Maybe at noon she could get a few winks of much-needed sleep at her desk.

This particular morning, Lewis Larson had decided to help the teacher build a fire in the school's pot-bellied stove. It was a cold day, and the room surely would be uncomfortable when they arrived. A school board member, Mr. Nelson, had recently hauled in a load of coal sufficient to last to the end of the winter. The coal was stored in a bin in the entryway. Next to the bin was a wooden box of kindling wood and old newspaper to use when starting a fire in the stove. The entryway was also where the children hung their wraps.

When they arrived at the school, it was already warm. Someone had come in early and started a fire in the stove. The children had begun to filter into the school from the nearby farms of the western Minnesota rural community. All sixteen of the children were in attendance. It was warm and cozy in the room for the students as they began reading their assignments, drawing, coloring pictures, and visiting with each other. The conversations were in English, as Miss Wilson had asked her students to speak only English when in the classroom. The native languages spoken by this year's children were ten Swedish/Norwegian, two German, two Polish, and two Danish.

"Who built the fire in the stove?" Lewis inquired as he stopped the sleigh in front of the schoolhouse.

Carrie suddenly had a worried look on her face as she responded in a quiet and wavering voice, "I wonder."

Lewis saw the concerned look on the teacher's face and began looking around. He checked around the perimeter of the schoolhouse but saw no person, then he checked inside the two outhouses along either side of the school building. His search made him even more suspicious and somewhat worried. He had thoughts of staying a few hours as a precaution, but he was already behind in his chores and projects back at the farm.

Just before the class began, Lewis began the return trip to the farm to resume the daily chores he had started at five in the morning. He and another son, Theodore, were in the process of building onto the windmill pump house. Lewis Larson was unaware of how the events of the day would alter the life of his children's teacher and his own family.

Miss Carrie walked to the entryway to get some coal for the stove. When she returned, a strange man followed her to her desk. He took off his coat, hat, and rubbers, and sat down on a chair by the teacher's desk. He took a piece of paper and a pencil from off of the teacher's desk and began writing. He was the one who had built the fire, staying the night in the school's book closet. The children were unusually quiet as they watched the stranger closely. The atmosphere in the room was tense. Some of the older children sensed danger.

The day began with the Pledge of Allegiance. Everyone stood at attention, except the strange man. The children viewed this as odd since they were all taught that it was patriotic to stand at attention.

Miss Carrie continued the opening exercises with a reading from the Twenty-Third Chapter of the book of Psalms. It was out of sequence from the Book of Saint John where she had been reading. Some of the children immediately recognized this chapter from funerals they had attended. She read aloud in a nervous manner, her voice shaking and even breaking occasionally. The children sensed this unusual behavior from this normally confident and mild teacher.

The man kept writing without any pause of reflection or reverence for what the teacher was reading. He looked tired and anxious, as if he had stayed up all night worrying. He never looked at Miss Carrie, not even once. Two of the older boys felt that something bad was about to happen. When she had finished reading, she closed the Bible and began to pray. As she prayed she suddenly had a change in her demeanor. She seemed to relax and have a sense of peace about her as she prayed.

"Our Lord, we began this day by thanking You for bringing the children safely to school. Help the children with their lessons today and instill in them Your wisdom and love. Keep us safe from any harm. Send down Your guardian angels to protect us from harm and danger. Amen."

The prayer was unusually short from Miss Wilson's normal opening prayers. Some of the children had glanced at the man during the prayer and saw that he was unmindful and inattentive of Carrie's praying. The students sensed the request for angels as being very unusual. Miss Wilson had never prayed this before. When the children opened their eyes, they were all affixed on the man.

For the next hour and a half, Carrie went through the day's assigned lessons, concentrating especially on those children who were struggling with learning a language other than their parents' native language. All eight grades were being taught to the sixteen children in attendance.

Soon it was time for recess. Because it was so cold, everyone stayed in the schoolroom instead of going outside. The man got off the chair, put on his coat, cap, and rubbers, and went out to the entryway. Carrie followed him with the coal bucket. All of the children wondered who this man was.

The cumulative recess noise was suddenly broken by some loud arguing and an unusually sharp noise from the entryway that sounded like something falling to the entryway floor. It was the coal bucket filled with coal that had fallen, but that was only part of the sound. A couple of the older boys who were familiar with guns immediately recognized a gunshot as the other part of the strange sound. "That's a gun," the boys uttered, one in the Norwegian language and the other in the Swedish language.

Miss Wilson suddenly burst into the room. "Help me, boys! He has a gun and is shooting at me!" She was bleeding from her left earlobe. She ran around the desks to the opposite side of the room. The strange man entered the school room with his five-shot revolver still smoking. He had his coat pocket full of bullets and was ready to reload when necessary. He shot again across the room, just missing Carrie and striking the blackboard.

One of the boys daringly stuck his foot out and tripped the man, which proved to be a dangerous thing to do. The man fell, causing his gun to discharge again. The bullet just missed young Molly Peterson, who was sitting near the big world globe, and pierced the picture of George Washington on the wall. As the shooter was getting up from the floor, Carrie was able to run out of the school.

"Children, get out of the school and go home!" the man yelled in a voice that sounded like he was crazed. He then sprinted out of the schoolhouse to chase after the teacher.

The children hesitated until the man left the school. One of the girls saw him running after Carrie outside as she looked through a window. "He's gone," she yelled out, "let's go." The children jumped from their seats and poured out of the school in the direction of their homes. One of the boys started toward a nearby farmhouse where he knew a phone had recently been installed. Some of the children were so scared that they ran off without taking their winter wraps. This was a mistake.

Carrie had run out of the school and across the road to the Zion Lutheran Church. The man pursued her, shooting once and then stopping to reload his gun with bullets from his pocket. She ran up to the church door to get inside. *Maybe I can lock myself inside,* she thought. The door was locked. It was usually unlocked. The pastor of the church had begun locking it since someone had recently entered and stolen some eating utensils from the kitchen.

Another shot pierced the church door as Carrie turned to run once more. A few seconds later another shot rang out and broke a church window. He fired several times more. Carrie's mind was frantic and racing. What could she do to keep from getting shot? She thought of the children inside the school. *Did they all get out safely? Did any of them get shot?* she wondered. She ran around the church turning once and noticing the man was not far behind. Once again he stopped to reload his gun, which gave Carrie a chance to gain some distance on him.

The man was of stocky build and medium height, and he moved much slower than the fleet-footed young teacher. Carrie once again ran across the road and into the school, where she was relieved to see that all the children were gone.

Carrie's assailant momentary lost track of her and stopped. He reached into his coat pocket and lifted out the handful of remaining bullets and counted them. He began to walk toward the school across the road and in pursuit of his victim—his former girlfriend Carrie Wilson.

Meanwhile all of the children were in various fields and roads on their way to their homes or a classmate's farm. It was more than a mile across the field to the Larson farm. The Rosen-quist children were running with the Larson children. Little Louise Larson was scared and crying as she ran through the fall-plowed field. Her big brother Freddie picked her up and carried her, shielding her face from the cold wind. He wrapped her in his sheepskin coat that he had managed to grab as he ran out of the school. She was also wearing his gloves.

Once again, a shot rang out from the gunman. He had found Carrie on the backside of the school. He shot once again, and almost at the same time there was a groan from the teacher. She had taken a second bullet. Carrie ran around to the front of the school, blood still running down her neck from her earlobe. She wasn't sure where the second bullet had pierced her body, but she was feeling a burning pain in her chest.

The disturbed man ran around to the front of the school and yelled out, "Where are you, Carrie? If I can't have you, nobody's going to have you. We will both go together!" Carrie recognized those words as the same words he had used in his letter.

The shooter saw his target move from behind the outhouse. He fired his gun and once again a bullet hit Carrie, this time in her jaw. Carrie knew he needed to reload his gun and she made a break for the churchyard once again. She remembered her school days when she won all of the foot races she ever entered. The pain was starting to affect her agility and speed, but she knew she needed to put some distance between her pursuer and herself. And quickly! She even thought about running to the farm across the field.

Carrie managed to get to the churchyard before the man spotted her. He ran to the front steps of the church and spotted Carrie's long dress behind a tree. The man shot his gun three more times, thinking he would hit her with quick random shots. This time the bullets all missed Carrie with one of them ricocheting off a stone protruding out of the ground. Carrie had been hit at least three times and the blood was beginning to soak through large portions of her clothes. She headed back to the schoolhouse.

The Larson children—Roy, Freddie, Joe, and little Louise—were still running across the fall-plowed field along with the Rosenquist children. The wind was blowing from the south causing the skin to start to freeze on their exposed hands and faces. They soon reached the creek and crossed it on the makeshift board crossing.

Carrie continued to attempt to dodge the bullets that were whizzing past her. In his pursuit of her the man started to fatigue, which caused him to become unbalanced and unsteady in his aim with the gun. He was also slipping on the snow-covered ground. Carrie ran in an unpredictable zigzagging pattern so as to make herself a more difficult target for her assailant. He had placed sixteen bullets in his coat pocket before he left the hotel the day before, which he would load into the five-chamber pistol as needed.

Carrie took a fourth bullet in her shoulder as she once again approached the now-emptied country schoolhouse. Her run had slowed to a walk because of the pain and blood loss. She thought if she could reach the doorway of the school, she could block the door and hide somewhere inside. "Maybe I can hit him with the baseball bat standing in the corner," she encouraged herself out loud. The loss of blood was making her weak and lethargic.

As she was only a few feet from the front door, another bullet hit her in the back of her head. It toppled her and she sprawled on the ground, passing out for a moment. To her former boyfriend she appeared dead. The uncontrollable assassin, tired from the chase, looked at his victim and shouted. "I think you've had enough, Carrie!"

Carrie, barely conscious, lay still, thinking he would use his gun once more to make sure she was dead. Shaking uncontrollably, he shot once more. He was aiming for her head, but he hit her in the thigh. With only one bullet left, he backed away from Carrie a few steps and stood looking at her for a full minute. He then reached into his pocket once more, retrieved his last bullet, and loaded it into his empty gun chamber. With the stature of a trained soldier, he stood up straight and put the gun horizontally to the side of his head. Then he squeezed his eyes shut tight and pulled the trigger. Carrie opened her eyes in time to see his last movements on the ground. She had thought that the last shot was going to be for her. "It's over," she muttered in pain. "Thank You, God."

Carrie lay still on the ground for about two minutes without observing any more movement from the man. She could see the blood running from his head onto the snow-covered, frozen ground. "I just hope he made his peace with the Lord," she said out loud.

Carrie could feel nothing in her legs or feet. She knew that some of the bullets that had penetrated her body—she didn't know how many—had done some damage. Her attempts to move her legs were unsuccessful. She dragged herself into the now-abandoned schoolhouse with her arms and hands, leaving a trail of blood on the entire way floor. All she could think of was getting herself close to the warm stove in the middle of the room. She was cold, scared, and shaking and she was quickly losing blood.

By now the Larson children had reached their farmhouse and hastily told the rest of the family of the horrible ordeal. Some of the Larson and Rosenquist children had frostbitten fingers and ears. Older sisters Lena and Esther Larson rubbed snow on them to help keep them from sustaining permanent damage. By now little Louise had stopped crying. Joe and Roy were trying to get warm using quilts from the sofa in the living room.

Theodore and Freddie quickly jumped into the sleigh that had been used to carry the teacher and the children to school only a few hours earlier, and headed back to the school. Theodore was very worried about Carrie. He had become Carrie's self-appointed protector since the day she arrived at the Larson farm in September 1912. A neighbor who had found out about the shooting from his own children stopped by to do what he could. The trip to the schoolhouse was made in record time. Even the horse Nelly seemed to understand the urgency of the moment.

When Theodore and Freddie arrived at the school, they saw the man lying in a pool of blood in front of the school. They saw the trail of blood leading into the school. Both Freddie and Theodore assumed the worst for the teacher. They ran into the schoolhouse and found Carrie sitting next to the stove propped up next to her desk and crying uncontrollably. Some of the other parents had gotten the news and were starting to arrive at the school also.

Lewis and the neighbor arrived minutes after Theodore and Freddie. They all quickly tried to stop the bleeding from Carrie's bullet wounds with the use of clean towels from underneath the washbasin cabinet. All of the parents were shocked by how many times she had been hit by bullets and wondered how many were still in her body.

Lewis asked Carrie in the Norwegian language, "Did you know this man?"

She stopped crying for a moment and answered him in Norwegian in a weak, subdued voice, "He is from my past. Yes, I did know him. I am so sorry."

By this time, more parents of the children had reached the school. They gave further aid to Carrie who was shivering violently with cold. A couple of the mothers placed a thick, soft blanket on the floor and helped Carrie lie down on it, then they gently placed a pillow under her head. They continued in their attempt to stop the bleeding from the numerous places where she had been hit.

A couple of the nearby farmers found a horse blanket in the barn and covered the body of the shooter lying outside the school. The sight was gruesome. He was a complete stranger to everyone. It would be up to the county coroner to find out where to send the body.

Lewis and Theodore very carefully carried Carrie out to the neighbor's sleigh and placed her on some blankets they had taken from inside the school. The blankets were provided to the school by the township in the event bad weather required the children to stay overnight. On the trip back to the Larson farmhouse, the neighbor drove the team and Lewis attempted to stop further blood loss from Carrie's wounds. Freddie and Theodore drove Nelly and sleigh back to the farm.

Two of the children who had run out of the school had run to a nearby farm that had a phone. The police in Moorhead were alerted, as well as a doctor and the hospital. The sheriff and coroner would soon arrive at the school.

Lewis suspected that one of the bullets must have caused Carrie's inability to move her legs. He wondered if further damage might have been done when they had moved her to the sleigh or during the bumpy ride back to the farm on the frozen country roads.

Carrie was carefully moved into the Larson farmhouse and placed on the large dining room table where mother Jennie and daughter Lena had placed a heavy blanket. The Larson men and boys went outside to tend to Nelly, who had been pushed harder than normal on the trip to and from the school—twice in one morning.

Lena and Jennie carefully removed Carrie's blood-soaked clothes and placed them in a copper boiler filled with cold water. The bleeding from the gunshot wounds had nearly stopped. They counted six places where bullets had hit or penetrated her body. As they were washing the blood off of her skin and cleansing the wounds, Carrie spoke in a slurred and barely audible voice, "He shot his gun sixteen times when he was chasing me. For some reason I counted the shots. God was with me and an angel protected me. I saw the angel." Then she began to sob. "Are the children alright? Were any of them hurt at all?"

Mother Jennie placed her mouth down close to Carrie's ear and answered in her Swedish language, "As far as we know, they are all fine. Now you just relax, Miss Carrie." Carrie could speak both the Norwegian and Swedish languages fluently.

"Oh, thank you, Jennie," Carrie answered softly, "I was so worried." Jennie had become a second mother to Carrie since her arrival at the Larson farm the previous September.

After cleansing her body with warm soapy water, Jennie and Lena administered some antiseptic salve to Carrie's wounds to begin the healing process. The doctor and ambulance would be there soon. He would evaluate her condition, possibly remove any bullets, and decide what further treatment was needed. He might decide that removing any bullets on the farm dining room table may be too risky and wait to do it at the hospital. Both of the women knew that very likely there were some bullets remaining in her body that would need to be removed. The women carefully moved Carrie into the living room, placed her on the sofa, and covered her with a warm blanket. Carrie strained to speak.

"Don't talk now, Carrie," Jennie said quietly in a mixture of Swedish and English. "Just try to rest."

Mother Jennie prepared some herbal tea and helped Carrie to drink it. She was exhausted from the entire ordeal—the chase around the school and church yard, running in and out of the school, and finally from the cold and the loss of blood. All she wanted to do was sleep. She began to doze off, thinking that she may never wake up again. She knew she was ready to meet her Maker, if that were the case.

She began to dream of her childhood back in Massachusetts. The warm herbal tea and her need for sleep gave her some soothing relief from her pain.

Chapter 2

July 4, 1888

*C*arrie Mildred Wilson was born in Springfield, Massachu-setts, on July 4, 1888, into a well-to-do family. Her parents were both from families that had immigrated to the United States from Europe—her mother Molly from Ireland, and her father Oleg from Norway. The town where Oleg was born was on the Swedish border, and he taught Carrie both the Norwegian and Swedish languages at an early age. Molly was Catholic and Oleg was Lutheran. Unlike most of the immigrants to America, both families were wealthy—her dad in the wholesale food business and her mom's family in the import-export business. They both wanted the best for their daughter. Carrie could speak English, Norwegian, and Swedish well by the time she was in the fourth grade.

From an early age, Carrie could see the socioeconomic divi-sion in the people who populated the various neighborhoods in Springfield. Many of the well-to-do families had little con-cern for the poor. The poor could only wish to have the mate-rial wealth, sufficient food, and the opportunities that America promised to give them.

The Wilsons lived on a hill above the railroad tracks. Carrie would frequently sit on the green grassy hill and watch the chil-dren play in the streets and vacant lots across the tracks. Often she wished she could be with them playing. Sometimes she would ask her mother to take her over the tracks to play with the children. She was always told 'no' for various reasons—sometimes without a reason being given at all.

It was at an early age that Carrie began to dream at night—dreams that she most often had the ability to remember later in vivid detail. She also formed the habit of writing the dreams on paper soon after she woke up. By the time she was a teenager, she had a large collection of nighttime dreams. There was usually one every night and occasionally more than one.

She was sent to a private school in the first grade. She excelled in math, reading, and science. From early on, her parents could see that Carrie was destined to become a doctor or a lawyer. At least that was their plan was for her. Unfortunately, Carrie's own dreams and plans were not the same as her parents' dreams.

When she was in the second grade, Carrie's class went on a field trip one afternoon. They toured the big railroad roundhouse just across the tracks from where she lived. For some reason, she got lost during the tour and missed the horse-drawn school buggy at three. She decided to walk home to the other side of the tracks and up the hill. As she walked, she passed children playing on the sidewalks and in the vacant lots and streets. She passed some girls who were jumping rope. Carrie could see they were not very good at this activity; Carrie was an expert at it. Because there were very few children in her neighborhood, jumping rope was one activity that she could do alone. She did it often, and she did it very well.

"Come jump rope with us," one of the girls called out as Carrie walked by. The girl had long black hair that looked like it hadn't been combed for many days. Her speech had an accent to it. Carrie had been told by her dad that there were many Italian immigrants in that community. Their fathers worked at various jobs on the railroad.

Carrie hesitated for a moment, remembering what her parents would often tell her. "Be careful to not associate with the children on the other side of the tracks. They are poor and not well-behaved. They will lead you down many wrong roads."

Finally, one of the girls walked over to Carrie and handed her a rope. Carrie could see that it wasn't really a jump rope purchased in a store. It appeared to be a portion of a dog lead that had been cut to a length that was just right to jump.

Carrie walked over to where the girls were jumping. They all looked as she began to jump. Soon she was doing all sorts of fancy moves that caused the girls to stare at her with mouths agape. "Will you teach us some of those moves?" one of the girls asked.

"Sure," Carrie said happily.

Meanwhile, back at the school Carrie did not appear off the buggy after the field trip. Molly became frantic, imagining all sorts of horrible situations. She talked to the driver, and he agreed to go back to the roundhouse and look for Carrie. Molly went along.

By this time, Carrie was teaching one of the girls to jump doubles. Her mother was the first to see the girls, but assumed that Carrie wouldn't be with them. "Carrie has been warned about associating with this trash," she said out loud.

"There she is!" the buggy driver yelled out.

"Where?" Molly asked.

"With those girls," he replied.

"Oh, my goodness!" she said almost hysterically.

The horse-drawn buggy was soon only a few feet from where the girls had stopped jumping. "I need to go, girls," Carrie told them.

They all thanked Carrie for showing them new rope-jumping techniques, and each took a turn giving her a hug. "Come back again so we can jump rope some more," they said almost in unison in their Italian-accented voices.

What happened next, Carrie would never forget, and it turned her against her mother. Molly grabbed Carrie's hand and jerked her up into the buggy. Then she slapped Carrie—not once but twice across her mouth. Carrie began to cry. Her new friends saw what was happening, and some of them began to cry at the cruel punishment they had just witnessed.

The buggy driver looked at Carrie's mother and could not help but comment, "Isn't that an awfully cruel thing to do to your daughter . . . and embarrassing for her?"

"Carrie, I have told you repeatedly not to associate with these riffraff. When you get home, I want you to take a good long bath," Molly admonished, ignoring the comments of the buggy driver.

The driver drove off. Carrie sobbed all of the way home. She had known that her mother had a cruel streak, but this action was beyond normal parental discipline. Her mother tried to talk to Carrie, but she just kept her face pointed toward the window and said nothing.

When they arrived at their home, the carriage driver could not help himself. "I'm glad I didn't have you for a mother. That would have been a nightmare."

Carrie took a bath and went to her room. Even at this young age, she began yearning for the day when she would be leaving her unhappy home. She stayed in her room all night. The next morning Carrie never spoke to her mother. She knew her mother believed she was acting in what she thought was the best interests of her daughter, but Carrie was angered by those actions. *Aren't there other methods of correction?* She thought. Carrie decided that she would never forgive her mother.

* * * * *

1900

There was almost constant conflict between Carrie and her mother. This conflict was evident from an early age. Molly wanted Carrie to become either a lawyer or a doctor. Carrie's first ambition was to become a teacher of children. Her second dream was to become a nurse. But this difference in career goals with her mother was only part of the conflict between them. Carrie was a very talented girl and her mother always wanted to show her off to her society friends. When her mother visited her friends, she would drag Carrie along to show her off to them. Carrie just wanted to live a happy childhood and teen life with friends of her own choosing.

Carrie continued to record her dreams. They had to do with various subjects. She soon had several diaries filled with dreams. Her mother would often ask her what she planned to do with these books of dreams. "I don't know, Mother. Maybe I'll write a book someday," she would answer.

Molly would have only one response: "Stupid!"

Oleg became Carrie's role model and hero at an early age. He was the parent who did take her to jump rope and play other games with the Italian and other immigrant children on several occasions. Some of these children even invited Carrie to their birthday parties. She developed a passion for several things—athletics, the study of ethnic cultures, history, and reading.

In her mind, Carrie's mother was a social climber—she had to constantly be at the top of the socioeconomic hierarchy. She had no concern for others unless it helped her to achieve her goal of being on top. She was concerned with wealth and all of the social status it brought with it. Most of all, she seemed completely devoid of any genuine love and concern for her only child, Carrie.

This characteristic of Carrie's mother greatly affected Carrie's personality during her teen years. She would wish to do things and associate with people who were just the opposite of her mother. Oleg recognized this conflict and purposely stayed clear of getting involved. He attempted to help them resolve their differences but gave up once he realized Carrie would grow up to be a wonderful caring woman. He knew he couldn't change his wife.

In the seventh grade Carrie noticed that the boys received most of the attention and opportunities in organized sports. She had experienced a rapid growth spurt over the summer and was now a tall, strong young woman. One fall afternoon shortly after school dismissed for the day, she found her gym teacher on the football field. He was also the football coach and was about to commence practice. "Tell me, Mr. Gordon, what competitive sports does this school have for girls to participate in?"

The muscle-bound man of forty was taken up short by the spunky co-ed's direct question. He stopped what he was doing and looked at Carrie. "What is your name?" he asked.

"Carrie Wilson," she replied.

"Well, Carrie Wilson, normally we think of only boys as being involved in sports. The girls usually are interested in the activities that are traditionally for the ladies. . . like sewing, cooking, and the like."

Carrie expected that answer and was about to counter the coach's statement with her practiced response.

"However," he continued without giving her an opportunity to speak, "I am of a different opinion. I believe that girls need to have the same opportunity to participate in competitive athletics as boys. I have tried to get our school board to permit some competition for the girls, but the 'powers that be' refuse to listen."

Carrie saw an opportunity to further the discussion and convince the "powers that be" that women could be athletic just as men. "Maybe we can demonstrate to the board that we girls can run, jump, and compete just as well as the boys," she confidently responded.

The coach thought for a moment. He had long hoped that an opportunity would sometime present itself. He believed that the right athletic young woman would handily show what women can do in the hundred-yard dash, the low and high hurdles, and other track events. Maybe this was that time. The coach looked at his pocket watch and snapped it shut. "Let me see you run in the hundred. Our fall track practice is about to start over on the other field. I will ask the track coach if you can run with the boys."

"Thank you," Carrie replied.

After talking to the track coach, Carrie was permitted to run the warm-up laps around the field with the boys. Because of her physical beauty, she was somewhat of a distraction to the boys who were very surprised to have a girl running next to them.

The boys were all in high school and were of the opinion that Carrie was also in high school. No one had told them otherwise.

Meanwhile, Oleg was at the school to give Carrie a ride home and saw what was going on. Fortunately, he was of the same opinion as the coaches on the lack of opportunity for women to have competitive physical programs as part of their education. He stood back and just watched. It was also fortunate that Carrie's father was picking her up from school this particular day, as it was usually her mother who had this duty.

"Okay, Carrie Wilson. Let's see what you can do," the track coach said to her. He had watched her run in her gym class the previous spring and wondered how she would do in a race against the boys. He was really surprised to see her after her summer growth spurt. "George, Ted and Tony . . . line up for a race around the track."

Carrie suddenly felt a little nervous. She wasn't expecting this opportunity to run with the boys, let alone run on the school track.

The boys walked up to the starting marks. Carrie was the last to get to her mark. Just as suddenly as it had started, all of the nervousness vanished from her. She got down on one knee and focused on a tree in the next lot beyond the school property. She knew she would need to beat these boys in a convincing manner to make an impression on those watching.

Two members of the school board just happened to be at the track to watch their own sons training. The football coach walked over to them and explained what was going on. The three of them agreed that if the school was to embark on girls' competitive athletics, Miss Carrie would need to perform well on this one race.

"On your mark . . . get set . . ." Bang! Went the starter pistol that the track coach aimed into the air. The four runners took off.

Carrie was long-winded and had long legs. She burst forth into the lead immediately. The boys she was racing were not only overly confident but also slightly hesitant about beating the young woman. She was way out in front by the end of the race.

The boys were very surprised at both her speed and her age. Most of them were also taken off guard by her beauty. They were more interested in how they could vie for her affections than how to beat her in a race.

Everyone congratulated Carrie. They were all wondering what the next test for this energetic young female would be. As if reading their minds, Carrie answered their question with another question. "How about running a long-distance race?"

There was a quiet moment from the group of male onlookers.

"Let's do it. Let's do the four-forty," the track coach blurted out. "Let's get three more boys on the track." The coach selected three of the faster runners he had on his team to run this race. He was willing to run the risk of his boys beating Carrie and destroying her chances of going further with her young running career. But he knew the only way Carrie would be able to help launch a women's athletic program would be for her to win against the best runners. He was that confident in her talent after seeing her run.

Soon all four runners were at their marks on the seven-lane track. Carrie was on the inside lane. The track coach walked in front of the runners. "Okay, you guys . . . I do *not* want you to hold back just because you're running against a girl. Give it all you've got." He stepped to the side and raised his starter pistol once more. Once again Carrie became nervous, and once again she knew that being nervous was part of any competition. It motivated her.

Bang! At the sound of the gun they all took off. Carrie knew that any race is not won in the first few seconds, but in the last few. She got off to a quick start but then slowed down to keep pace with the leader. Soon she was out in front with her long legs stretched out in front of her like an African gazelle. She kept running at an ever-increasing pace and finished twenty feet ahead of the fastest boy in the school. The crowd which by this time had grown to include all of the teachers still at school, roared excitedly. Again, everyone congratulated Carrie.

The next day the track coach told Carrie that not only would she be allowed to compete on the track team, but also she could compete in any post-season state competition. Oleg was happy for her. Molly was furious, but Carrie expected that from her mother. She went on to win medals in the hundred-yard dash, the 220, the 440, the low hurdles and the high hurdles—all in the seventh grade while competing at the high school level. The track coach was able to enter her in the boys' competition without any protest. No other school had any girls' track program.

Everyone expected Carrie to go on to have a successful career in track. But there was just one problem: her school was one of only a handful in the state that had a women's athletic program. A track career was not to be for Miss Carrie.

Carrie excelled in school. She now was interested in science, math, history, and social studies, along with reading. When she was a senior, she was able to take some college courses for credit and received A's in everything. She was all set for her college education.

She was selected as the Queen of the Spring Ball her senior year. Her escort was the son of the mayor of Springfield. It was her first official date in all of high school. She was a very beautiful and attractive young woman, but she was also a very modest person and did not dwell on her beauty. She carried that attitude into her college years and beyond.

Carrie read her Bible and prayed often. She attended a church down the street from her house and became involved with the youth, taught Sunday school, and helped with the neighborhood food program. Unfortunately, Carrie's mother and father did not attend any church.

* * * * *

1906

Just as she had in high school, Carrie excelled in her college education. It was an escape from the control that her mother desired to have over Carrie. This unquenchable desire to control irritated Carrie's father, and it wasn't long before her parents separated. They decided not to divorce due to the reduction of wealth the action would have caused. Their marriage was reduced to little more than a business partnership.

Carrie's parents' marriage had been arranged by their parents and had always been a loveless union. Carrie could see this from an early age. This marriage, devoid of love, had pulled Carrie's folks apart. Added to this problem was the continual conflict between Carrie and her mother.

Her father had it all set up to have Carrie attend a pre-medical school where she would be the first woman student. Her grades were almost perfect when she graduated from high school, thus making it easy for her to be accepted. Carrie was sure to excel in what sports were available for the women to participate in. Running was her main interest, and her high school coach had suggested she may wish to try out for the Olympics. She decided against that.

Over the summer months Carrie spent time alone at the family summer lake home in Connecticut. She ran and swam every day and had a part-time job at a variety store. This was the only time Carrie was able to talk to her parents in an amenable manner. She knew she should forgive her mother for the traumatic occurrence in the second grade, but her anger just would not allow it. She kept it hidden deep inside of her. It was a root of bitterness that was being watered and nurtured by time. Carrie could not let go of it, although she knew she had to some day.

It was during that summer in Connecticut while swimming one afternoon that she met Michael Jenkins. He was a quiet young man who was also from a well-to-do family. His father was a lawyer and had extensive business holdings. Carrie met the family one night at a neighborhood gathering. All those in attendance were from the upper class of the community. She accompanied Michael to several social and athletic events over the summer. Many times Michael's parents and brothers and sisters would be present at those gatherings.

As the summer progressed, Michael began to exert a possessive behavior toward Carrie. She had noticed early on that he seemed to be overly controlling of her, and as time went on there was a seemingly deep-seated psychotic element to his personality. In late summer he displayed another behavior that Carrie found particularly disturbing. They were at a carnival where he was playing a game of chance and displaying his obvious addiction to gambling. In this case, he was losing.

Carrie took him by the arm and attempted to steer him to another part of the carnival, but he violently pulled his arm away from her. He yelled at her in a voice that mirrored his frustration, "No! I just need to try it once more and see if I can win!"

He tried it once more with the same outcome—losing. Carrie explained, "Michael, it doesn't matter how many times you play this game. You'll never win back what you've lost because the game is fixed. That's how these things work."

Michael turned to the vendor running the Tent of Chance with fire in his eyes and fists clenched. He said in a very threatening and irrational tone, "I ought to beat you to a pulp or kill you. This game isn't fair."

With that Carrie turned away and began to walk to the exit. That was enough of Michael! She wanted nothing more to do with him. She went home and wrote Michael a letter terminating their relationship. She thought that it would be the end of their relationship and any further contact she might have with him.

* * * * *

Against her father's wishes and plans, Carrie enrolled at a teacher's college in Pennsylvania. The school was near an Amish community, and Carrie was at once attracted to the people and their culture. In one of her classes in high school, her teacher had given her an assignment to write about the Amish. She researched the subject with great passion and received a high mark from the instructor. Now she could possibly get to meet and become acquainted with these fine people.

Her father was not pleased with Carrie's choice of school. Her mother did not voice approval or disapproval. They were not very close after the episode in the second grade. Carrie could not forget the way her mom embarrassed her that day and then physically hurt her. She doubted that her mother even remembered that particular incident, but Carrie couldn't forget it and thought about it almost every day.

Oleg followed Carrie through her three years of college. He fully expected her to go on to further education, hopeful she would become a doctor. Carrie secretly had other plans and kept those plans to herself until the Christmas before her graduation.

Carrie's father was the first to broach the subject while they were at the Christmas Eve dinner table. Molly had come to where her husband was currently living for the event. "What are your plans after you graduate this spring, Carrie?" Oleg asked.

Carrie was silent for a moment and then surprised both her parents. "I plan to teach schoolchildren at an Amish colony in Pennsylvania, if I can find a school that will accept a non-Amish teacher. I have the names of a couple of these schools."

Molly was immediately upset, since she had told her social friends otherwise. She had even gone so far as to name various prestigious graduate schools in New England. None of it was true, of course, and now Molly faced the embarrassment of having to confess the truth to her friends when they asked her about it. Her mother took it as a personal affront, and the division between mother and daughter intensified.

Carrie graduated at the top of her college class. Oleg had paid for her education up to that point with the hopes of talking her into going on to medical school. When Carrie refused to abide by her father's wishes he yelled out, "I am no longer going to finance any more of your education!" Carrie did not care. She now had all of the schooling she needed to teach children.

Carrie's parents refused to attend her college graduation. Carrie looked at her life up to that point as one of both happiness and sadness. *My future will have some happy moments and a few unhappy ones,* she reassured herself. *God will guide me in my future and all that He has planned for me.*

* * * * *

1909

Carrie applied for and received a position at one of the Amish schools to teach English to first and second graders. The school board even let her pick out the books she wanted to have the children read. The board approved the selection, of course.

Most people viewed the Amish dress and customs as being old-fashioned or perhaps even a little cultish. Carrie decided early in the school year to dress similarly and to honor the Amish customs, and she found an Amish home on the colony that would let her live there as long as she was teaching. One of the Amish women sewed some dresses and other clothes for her. Carrie also decided early on to visit the homes of her students so she could get to know their parents. She offered to teach English to the women, and many of them were happy for the opportunity to learn the language better.

Carrie taught at the colony for two years. During her second year she stayed with another family since her first host family had moved to a different colony over the summer. She learned more than her students. Her own mother never taught her how to cook, sew, garden, or wash clothes. Doing some of the work in the homes where she stayed was the only payment the families needed from her.

About halfway through her second year of teaching, Carrie was visited again by Michael Jenkins. Somehow, he had found out where she was teaching. She thought she had made it perfectly clear to him that she was through with him, and she was visibly irritated when he showed up at her school. He looked at her with a crazed look in his eyes, and she was very afraid of him. He looked at her as if he owned her; he had a very possessive personality. Carrie believed he was headed for a very unhappy and tragic life. He left without incident, and she wrote to him again asking that he not visit her anymore for any reason.

Although she was afraid of him Carrie felt somewhat safe and protected where she was staying. She had some frank discussions with the leaders of the colony about her situation. They informed all of the men in the colony to be alert for Michael, but it still did not eliminate the fear that she felt. *He could be lurking behind any tree,* she often said to herself. She was afraid of what he might do to her.

* * * * *

1911

At the end of her second year, Carrie applied for a job in a small country school in Apple, Ohio. She had answered an ad in a small town's newspaper. She did not want to leave her students at the Amish colony in Pennsylvania, but she desired to see more of the country to the west.

At her new school she was once again visited by Michael Jenkins. His possessive, menacing attitude toward Carrie was becoming increasingly psychotic. She told him directly to quit visiting her. Again, she asked the people she was staying with for protection. They advised her to call the police next time. She didn't think that would do any good unless he physically harmed her. She only wished to be left alone.

Just after Christmas in her year of teaching in Apple, she saw an ad in the local newspaper, *The Apple Pie Gazette.* It read:

> *Wanted: Female teacher for about 15 students to teach in rural western Minnesota country school. Room and board provided. Must be good at teaching English to children of immigrant parents. Also, willing to teach English to some adults on Saturday for extra pay. Contact Lewis Larson, Spring Prairie Township, Glyndon, Minnesota."*

Carrie cut out the ad and placed it in the book she was reading.

* * * * *

1912

Around the middle of March 1912, she was again visited by Michael. He found her in a small grocery store on a Saturday afternoon. On this occasion, he had been drinking and displayed very irrational and aggressive behavior. His eyes flashed with rage; they were bloodshot and bugging out of their sockets. During his visit, she purposely made sure she was in plain view of people. That was the only way she knew she would be protected. Carrie feared if he ever got his hands on her, he may eventually kill her. She needed to get away from him. This visit ended when she asked the owner of the store where the maple syrup was, which she knew was at the back of the store. Carrie excused herself from Michael and followed the owner to the back of the store. She hastily explained that she needed to get away from the man who was with her, and the owner escorted her into the back storage area and then out the back delivery door.

When she returned to her apartment that night, she wrote her final letter to Michael Jenkins:

> *Michael:*
>
> *Please do not visit me anymore. I cannot conceive of any common interests we may have between us. I am frightened by your possessive personality and erratic behavior, and just being in your presence makes me terribly uncomfortable. I believe you need psychiatric help, and I suggest you get some.*
>
> *Carrie*

That same night Carrie retrieved the ad for the teaching position in western Minnesota and applied. She mailed both letters the next day. It was time for her to move on once more.

At this time Carrie decided she was not interested in having any close male relationship. Many male acquaintances asked her for dates, but she always told them she was too busy teaching. The experience with Michael had wiped out her desire for any romance.

Only a week after mailing her application, Carrie received a brief reply from Lewis Larson of Spring Prairie Township in western Minnesota.

Miss Carrie:

Please come visit our school and talk with us about this position. Enclosed is a two-way train ticket to Stockwood where the train will stop. From there it is only six miles to our farm. You may stay with us. We have children who attend our school. One of my sons will be at the station to provide you with transportation to our farm.

Lewis Larson, Spring Prairie Township, Minnesota

She immediately wrote back and told Mr. Larson that she would make the trip at Easter break in two weeks.

The trip to western Minnesota was fascinating to Carrie. It was in the middle of April, and the farmers were in the fields plowing and planting their crops. Horses pulling various farm implements could be seen mile after mile from the train window. It was almost like the farms on the Amish communities.

She arrived at the small community of Stockwood at noon on a Saturday. The town was not very big—a post office, a general store, a small hotel and a bar. A man who looked like a young farmer held a sign with "Carrie Wilson" painted on it. They greeted each other and climbed onto a buggy pulled by a black horse. "My name is Freddie Larson, Miss Wilson. Welcome to Minnesota."

"Thank you very much," she replied.

They traveled about five miles together with Freddie pointing out the various farms and other points of interest. Arriving at the Spring Prairie Township, they stopped at the small white schoolhouse alongside the road. They walked inside for a short tour. Across the road was a white church. Carrie could see the name painted on a sign: Zion Lutheran Church. The church had a horse barn, which Freddie explained was shared by the school. "Many of the older students ride their horses to school," he informed her. "In the winter some of the students ride buggies and leave the horses in the barn during school hours."

He took Carrie on a tour of the area telling the history of the township and its people. It wasn't long before the two of them were speaking in the Norwegian language.

They soon were at the Larson farm where Carrie was the honored guest for the evening meal. Lewis Larson had two older sons who looked at Carrie as someone whom they would like to get to know a little better. Her beauty dazzled them. Only Jennie Larson noticed the looks in her sons' eyes. *I have no need to fear for my sons;* she said to herself, *she is much older than my sons. But it is not my sons I worry about; it's the husbands in the township that I worry about. Their wives will need to watch them closely. I have never seen a more beautiful woman in person.*

During the meal, Carrie gave a review of her family and home, education, teaching experience, and religious background. It was a family interview with all of the Larson children participating. For supper Jennie served Swedish meatballs and gravy, mashed potatoes, homemade brown bread, creamed carrots, and apple pie.

After the evening meal, Lewis and Jennie went for a walk down by the creek that ran through the Larson farmland. The children entertained Carrie by showing her around the farm. Since Lewis was the chairman of the school board, he decided to seek the opinion of his wife in making the decision whether or not to hire Carrie. The board had given him the authority to make the final decision.

The next morning at the breakfast table, Lewis voiced his offer to Carrie to teach at the Spring Prairie school beginning in the fall of 1912 at a salary of $78.00 per month. Carrie accepted immediately. Lewis was quick to add, "You may live with us free of charge if you are willing to help with some of the work around the farm, and we will provide you transportation to and from the school every day."

Later that afternoon Carrie happened to ask Jennie, "Where did you and your husband meet? You are Swedish and Mr. Larson is Norwegian, and the two countries don't usually mix. I know this from experience with my own family. Romances with people usually stay within their own nationality."

"We met during our employment at the Buffalo River Mansion," Jennie replied. "At first Lewis spoke very little English and I helped him with it. Of course, I was learning myself. Then one night we fell in love . . . just like that. That's another story. Sometime I will tell you the entire, romantic tale."

When Carrie returned to her home in Ohio, she informed the Apple school board of her decision to move west and teach. They were disappointed and wanted to keep her on for as long as she wanted. It was hard for her to leave the children and the nice people of the small community. She purposely did not share the details of her move fearing that her ex-boyfriend may try to find her once more.

Carrie began her teaching in the Spring Prairie Township country school in the fall of 1912. She stayed at the Larson home and fell in love with the Larson family immediately—especially the schoolchildren. They were well-behaved and very intelligent, some more than others. Carrie was very willing to help with chores, both inside the house and outside and with the animals. She also learned how to do some of the field work. The horses seemed to like Carrie.

She became a member of the Zion Lutheran Church after a month of attending. She became a Sunday school teacher, joined the Ladies Aid, and was a member of the Welcoming Committee.

Members of the opposite sex soon began to notice this very attractive young teacher. In some ways she loved the attention, but her first love was the teaching of her students. She was also fearful of another visit from her old boyfriend. She knew what may happen if he found her once again. She feared that day and did not know what she would do if it happened. Carrie also loved her job, her life with the Larson family, and she did not want anything to interfere with the life she enjoyed. She decided not to reveal her fears to the Larsons or to anyone else.

Somehow, Michael Jenkins managed to obtain her address at the Larson farm. When his letter showed up in March 1913, Carrie read it and stuck it in her night table drawer. She told no one about it.

Chapter 3

March 5th, 1913—2 P.M.

Four Hours After The Shooting

*A*t the Larson farm, Miss Carrie drifted in and out of consciousness until two in the afternoon. Mother Jennie and her daughter Lena gave her water and apple juice whenever she did stir. She was running a fever, but they kept her temperature to a reasonable level with wet washcloths. She had also lost a considerable amount of blood. It was about four hours after she had received the first bullet from the shooter. The mother and daughter team had suddenly become emergency nurses and were attending their patient with great love and care.

The Larson boys were on horseback waiting for the doctor and the horse-drawn, covered-wagon ambulance from Glyndon. They were stationed at the intersections going to the Larson farm driveway in case the ambulance driver did not know the way to the farm.

Upon his arrival, the doctor immediately began to examine Carrie. He decided the best thing for Carrie would be to have the bullets removed by a skilled surgeon at the hospital. The wounds had all stopped bleeding, thanks to the parents who first reached the school and the women at the farm. The doctor told the women that he was worried most about the bullet wound in the head.

"Could that prove fatal?" Jennie asked softly.

"Yes, it could," the elderly doctor answered. "It will take a surgeon more skilled than I to remove it. I just hope they have such a doctor at the hospital."

Carrie was placed on a stretcher and carefully carried out to the ambulance wagon. She was once again unconscious. Blankets were placed on the bed of the wagon, and more blankets were placed over Carrie. Along with the doctor, Mother Jennie and daughter Esther rode inside the wagon and continued to place cool, wet cloths on Carrie's head and neck to try to keep her fever down.

They made it to the railroad station in Stockwood just in time to place Carrie in the baggage car of the Northern Pacific passenger train, the next stop being Moorhead. From the Moorhead train station, she was transported to the Northwestern Hospital by a motorized ambulance. She arrived unconscious, and there was much speculation that she was not going to make it.

A team of doctors and nurses were ready to go to work on the patient. Advanced knowledge of the shooting had been communicated to the hospital staff, and they were ready with the doctors and equipment that they thought they needed.

The doctors quickly began to examine Carrie and prepared her for surgery to remove the bullets. The doctor chosen to remove the bullets was a young medical student from Iowa by the name of Dr. Andrew Peterson. He was in his last year of medical education at the University of Minnesota. He happened to be at Northwestern Hospital seeing two patients at the time Carrie was brought in. Since he was studying neurosurgery and had surgical experience, it was logical for him to be called in on this case.

Dr. Peterson was briefed on the situation and immediately went to work removing the bullets and applying the appropriate dressings to various wounds. His primary concern was the head wound, since it was in a critical location. After an hour of attempting to remove the bullet to the head, Dr. Peterson finally gave up. He was afraid that the procedure would do more harm than good. He needed to study the situation further and consult other surgeons before attempting to remove the bullet fragment.

Carrie remained unconscious for the next twenty-four hours. There were times when the doctors and nurses thought they were going to lose her. They monitored her vital signs, kept her temperature down, and kept her hydrated as best they could.

* * * * *

The local news media picked up on the story of Carrie's shooting incident and her condition. These reports were, in turn, picked up and spread by the national press. The news of the school shooting had quickly become a nationwide story. People wanted to keep track of the condition of the Minnesota country schoolteacher who had survived the shooting of sixteen bullets—six of them hitting their target. One report was from the *Moorhead Weekly:*

> *One bullet passed through the right mastoid back of the right ear, took a downward course and is lodged in the cervical vertebra at the base of the skull. Another bullet entered at the left of the nose and passed through the upper jawbone. This bullet has not been traced. Another bullet entered the chest to the left of the sternum and glanced off along the ribs and came out the back of the shoulder blade. The fourth bullet struck a glancing blow on the forehead but did not enter the skull. The fifth bullet entered the teacher's left thigh and was easily removed. The initial shot from the shooter was aimed directly at the teacher, but its deadly impact was deflected when she grabbed his hands just before he pulled the trigger. The bullet did pierce her left ear lobe and then lodged into the entry wall.*
>
> *Anti-tetanus serum was immediately administered to prevent lockjaw. The teacher has been heavily sedated and*

remains in shock, and in an unconscious state. It was Dr. Andrew Peterson's opinion at first that "the chances are against recovery, but this does not mean that there is no hope for recovery." Initially there was a report of a seventh bullet wound, but that was found to be incorrect.

—**Moorhead Weekly, March 6, 1913.**

Northwestern Hospital also issued a press release written by Dr. Peterson:

We have concluded that to remove the bullet in Miss Carrie Wilson's head would be potentially more harmful to her than if it was left where it is. The position of the bullet does not pose any serious long-term danger to her. As long as she receives regular checkups for any movement of the bullet, she may be able to live a normal life. We remain hopeful that one day, medical surgical advances will be developed that will allow the bullet to be removed safely. At this time she is still semiconscious and is receiving transfusions of blood. The bad news is that for some undetermined reason, she cannot move her legs or walk."

The news of the country school shooting and suicide continued to spread over the entire country with the public being both fascinated and concerned for the teacher and her condition. They viewed the story as a miracle. There were as many different stories of what exactly happened as there were people who had first- and second-hand knowledge of the incident.

The story of the assault upon Miss Wilson is variously told by different persons, but it seems that Michael Jenkins, twenty-four years of age, walked from Glyndon to Stockwood on Tuesday night and remained hidden there overnight. The school is only three miles north of Stockwood. He arrived there before school had started, broke into the building, and built the fire in the stove. As the school day was about to commence, Jenkins entered the schoolroom and surprised the teacher. Everything seemed to be agreeable between him and Miss Wilson, according to the students. At recess the two of them stepped into the coat hall and held a whispered consultation. Suddenly, Jenkins pulled his revolver and she seized his hands. A shot was fired and deflected, hitting Miss Wilson in her earlobe.

The teacher broke away from him and ran into the schoolroom. As he followed her, one of the boys tripped him. Miss Wilson ran out of the building and Jenkins, breaking away from the lad, followed her. It is thought that Miss Wilson's purpose in running from the school building was to get her assailant away from the children. For this reason, the people of the community believe she is a hero. She ran across the road toward the church, thinking she could hide there. It was locked so she ran around the building and back toward the school again, with Jenkins firing as he ran chasing her. She re-entered the school building. As Jenkins entered the school building behind her, he ejected the empty shells and reloaded his five-shot revolver. He fired across the empty room and missed.

When Miss Wilson again left the building, Jenkins followed her firing several times and reloading as he ran. They again ran toward and around the church and horse barn before returning back to the school building. He seems to have overtaken her near a small drift of snow in front of the school door and fired several shots at close range. Miss Wilson fell to the ground. It is presumed at that point Jenkins believed he had killed her. He put a bullet through his brain a short distance away from her, dying almost instantly. With her assailant dead, Miss Wilson crawled back into the schoolroom. One of the bullets had apparently rendered her unable to walk.

Letters found upon the person of the dead young man indicate he was in love with Miss Wilson, but that she declined to marry him for undisclosed reasons. The significant thing is that before leaving his home back east, he wrote a letter to his mother telling her what he was planning to do. He seems to have settled in his own mind that Miss Wilson's refusal to marry him at present was based on her love for another young man, and he deliberately made up his mind to kill her and himself. He wrote in the letter to his mother that his body would be found beside Miss Wilson's dead body. This letter was not mailed but was one of several found in Jenkins's coat pocket by coroner Arthur Burnett, who declined to give it out for publication in full.

* * * * *

Dr. Andrew Peterson was at the point in his career where he would choose his medical specialty. He had become interested in the subject of head injuries as a high school student when a good friend fell from the second story of a building while painting one summer. A brain bleed commenced, filling the head with blood. The doctors attempted to operate without any success. His friend died the following morning.

At that time Andrew was a senior in high school and decided to go into medicine after completing his college education. He remembered hearing one of his friend's doctors saying in the waiting room, "Someday, we hope we will have more knowledge and techniques to better operate on head injuries." Andrew believed he had the skill and the intelligence to be a successful pioneer in the field of neurosurgery.

Andrew was not sure whether or not Miss Carrie Wilson would have full cognitive function when she regained consciousness. It was possible she would be fine, or she may have pronounced loss of memory, a complete change in mood, constant pain, amnesia, or some other impediment to returning her to how she was before the shooting. The doctor was also afraid that a brain bleed might develop and cause permanent damage or death. The trauma of being shot in her schoolroom in front of her students, being chased around the school and church, and finally watching as her old boyfriend shoot himself in the head, could have a debilitating mental effect on her, as well. She also had some adverse effects from being chased through the snow and subzero wind chills, and the doctor was afraid she might develop pneumonia.

Doctor Peterson made the decision: to sit by his patient's bed and monitor her state of consciousness, temperature, blood pressure, and any other medically observable occurrence. He would record the data as he observed it as part of his research study. Also, he wanted to be there when she woke up. For a while he wasn't certain she ever would wake up. Many people came to the hospital to visit Carrie while she was unconscious. They were not allowed in to see her, of course. The nurses couldn't give any report on her condition since not even the doctors could define what it was other than unconsciousness and in guarded condition.

As he sat next to her bed, Andrew noticed the striking beauty of his patient for the first time. As an up-and-coming neurosurgeon, he had no interest in starting a romantic relationship with anyone, but for some reason he desired to get more acquainted with this miraculous survivor of a sixteen-bullet rampage from a jealous ex-boyfriend. Andrew considered her survival of this attack as nothing short of a miracle. He knew she must be someone very special. It was as if something or Someone had been protecting her. That Someone had now placed her partially in Andrew's hands.

Andrew continued his beside vigil for more than twenty-four hours, monitoring and charting her progress every thirty minutes. He was able to get a few winks of sleep from time to time. At one point, he drifted off to sleep and started to dream. He was walking hand in hand with his patient down a country road. Andrew woke up with a jolt, chastising himself for letting his mind drift into a romantic scenario with a patient he was treating. He tried to dismiss the dream as simply a reaction to extreme fatigue, but the thought of it kept coming back to him. *Impossible!* He told himself. *No credible doctor would ever pursue a romantic relationship with a patient. It's absolutely unprofessional and unthinkable!* He dozed off again, but this time he slept dreamlessly.

Late in the afternoon of Thursday, March 6th, Carrie began to wake up. At first Carrie's eyes opened slowly and blinked a couple of times. Andrew asked the attending nurse to give her some water and some juice. As Carrie tried to focus on her surroundings, she looked at Andrew and suddenly became alert. *Maybe she's thinking I'm the shooter, and she's afraid I'm going to try to shoot her one more time,* he thought.

Carrie laid her head back on the pillow and closed her eyes. In another few seconds, she again opened her eyes and this time, looked at the ceiling. She continued opening and closing her eyes for the next several minutes. Finally, she opened them for good, looked at Andrew, and quietly asked, "Who are you and where am I?"

This question told Andrew that Carrie was okay as far as her mind was concerned. "My name is Doctor Andrew Peterson, and I am one of the physicians who have been treating you. The good news is it appears you're going to live. Everyone has been very worried about you. You have survived a very traumatic event, and you have had a flock of visitors and well-wishers to see you. How do you feel?"

"I think I'm all right," Carrie answered. She raised her arms from off of the bed and wiggled her fingers. Then she attempted to raise her legs off of the bed, but she could not move them. With panic rising in her voice she asked, "Doctor, why is there no feeling in my legs?"

"Try to stay calm, Miss Wilson," the doctor answered. "We're not sure at this time exactly why you've lost the use of your legs. What do you remember about what happened to you?"

Carrie once more closed her eyes in an attempt to think about the traumatic events that had happened the previous morning. "It's coming back to me," she replied in a shaky voice. Then she placed her hands over her face and cried out mournfully, "Oh, no! What happened to the children? Did any of them get hurt?

The last thing I remember was running back to the school, and I was hit by a couple of bullets. Then I remember sitting inside the school, and then someone brought me back to the farm. That's all I remember."

Andrew did not need to worry about Carrie's memory. It seemed to be functioning properly—so far. "As far as I have been told, all of the children are fine," Andrew answered. "I was told that some of them had hands in various stages of frostbite. But I'm sure their parents took good care of them."

"How did they freeze their hands?" Carrie asked.

"I was told they ran away from the school to their homes for help," Andrew responded, "and some of the children weren't able to grab their coats. They were not dressed for the cold wind chill. But don't worry about any of that right now. You need to just rest and concentrate on getting well again. The trauma that you have been through has probably taken most of your energy. I need to get some rest and food myself."

Carrie looked at the doctor's clothes and hair. "Pardon me for saying so, but you look a little unkempt and wearied for a doctor."

Andrew responded, "Yes, I suppose you're right. I have been most interested in your case as I have not seen one like it before. I wanted to make sure I was here when you woke up so I could try to determine the extent of your injuries and their effects on your brain function."

"How long have I been here?"

"It's been almost twenty-four hours since I finished your surgery."

"Doctor, have you been sitting here all this time?" Carried asked unbelievingly.

"I have," he answered.

"Why would you do that?" she asked.

"To tell you the truth, I believe you are a living, breathing miracle. You have to be someone special to survive such a calamity. I have never had a patient like you in my brief career. I didn't realize it would take so long for you to regain consciousness, and I was very interested to know what was going on in your head from the bullet wound and the surgery. This is my field of medical study, and the information I got from monitoring your post-surgery recovery will be valuable to my research."

"Did I say anything or try to get up at any time?" Carrie asked.

"Not while I was here," the doctor answered. "But, I was out in the waiting room occasionally. So you may have recited the Gettysburg Address or done some cartwheels when I wasn't here to witness it."

"I don't think so, doctor," Carrie replied with her first brief smile.

Carrie slept soundly through the night, thanks in part to large doses of pain medication and her body's extremely fatigued condition. The next morning she was given a breakfast of toast, orange juice and tea. Sometime around mid-morning, Andrew walked in. Carrie noticed his clean-shaven and rested condition. "Hey, you cleaned up very well, Doctor," she commented.

"Thank you, patient," he responded, trying unsuccessfully to stifle a yawn. "Let's see if your mind is as stable this morning as it was yesterday. Tell me your life's story . . . the short version. Where you were born? Where you went to school?—about your parents, that sort of thing . . . all the important stuff. If you get tired, just stop and rest your head."

Carrie thought for a moment and then slowly and in a slurred manner of speaking proceeded to share her life's story. "I was born in New England and educated there." At that point Carrie had tears in her eyes as she looked at Andrew.

"Why the tears?" Andrew asked. "You should be happy you're alive."

"I have no idea," Carrie answered, "Perhaps they are tears of happiness in answer to my prayer for God's protection. Maybe it's a reaction to the medication the nurses have given me."

Carrie continued and completed her story, occasionally resting her head on the two soft pillows. It took her no more than three minutes to give the doctor the condensed version of her personal history.

"I guess my story is both happy and sad. I had a sad time with my mother but a happy time with my dad. I have had a happy time with my teaching career but a sad time with my relationships. Now this! That's the story of my life . . . the short version."

"Perhaps sometime you can fill me in with all of the details," Andrew responded with a wink and a smile.

Carrie returned her head to her pillow. She wasn't sure how to respond to Dr. Peterson's comment. Perhaps he was like all the other single young men in her life—interested in one thing only. Or perhaps he was just a friendly young doctor, unlike the other "stuffed shirt" doctors Carrie had known. Carrie adamantly resolved anew to have nothing to do with romance, especially in light of the events of the past forty-eight hours. If it became necessary, she would make that clear to the good doctor.

As she closed her eyes, Andrew stepped out to the nurse's station to tell the head nurse, "Carrie is still with us, fully conscious, and in good spirits. You'll need to give her some additional blood, and keep giving her morphine as needed."

Later that afternoon, Andrew stopped by Carrie's room once more to check on her. She was resting when he walked into the room, but she became fully alert as soon as he reached her bedside.

"Doctor, can you please find me a piece of paper and a pencil?" Carrie asked. "I need to write down the dream that I had when I was unconscious. The Lord answered my prayer and performed a miracle on me. I believe I was dead for a short time, and I actually talked Him into giving me back my life when I told Him my students needed me."

Andrew studied Carrie for a moment and then finally said, "Carrie, that sounds like just a dream. You were unconscious for over twenty-four hours. I will get some writing tools for you, but I wouldn't put much stock in what you dreamed."

"You don't believe me do you, Doctor?" Carrie replied.

"I've heard of this phenomenon before, and many people have had this same type of dream. But let's not worry about that now. Writing is probably a good exercise for you at this point anyway." Andrew decided it was pointless to try to convince Carrie that she had just been dreaming. He thought it best to simply let her come back to reality on her own. He complied with her request for paper and a pencil, and he also found her a clipboard to make it easier for her to write.

Carrie was alone in the room as she closed her eyes and began to recall the ordeal she had just been through. As she thought, she remembered and wrote down the dream she had experienced.

I clearly recall that I felt a sense of weightlessness and was lifted up in the air. I was suddenly in a beautiful garden with flowers I had never seen before. Two angels came to me, took my hands, and led me to a Man in a white robe. The Man, Who I know was Jesus, told me I had been a good servant and welcomed me to go with Him. I asked Him, "Where are you taking me?" He never answered me, but I assumed it was heaven.

Suddenly, I felt a sense of urgency to return to the living. I told Him, "Lord, what will become of the children You have given me to teach? Is that not one of the purposes for which You created me? I am not yet done teaching. Might I go back and finish the work You have given me to do?"

The Lord looked at me with the most loving eyes I have ever seen. It was almost as if I could reach out and touch the love as it left His eyes and penetrated mine. He smiled at me and said, "You have chosen well, My daughter. You will be returned to your life, and you will teach the children again. You will go through a recovery period and will someday walk again. Just be patient and listen to your doctor. He will be your close friend for the rest of your life on earth."

The two angels once again took my hands and led me to a place where I felt gravity once more. It pulled me down and I went into the deepest of sleeps again.

—*Carrie Wilson—March 7, 1913.*

Perhaps I will show this sheet to Dr. Peterson later, she said to herself, *and then maybe he will believe me.* She wondered what Andrew's spiritual background was and whether or not he went to church. Then she caught herself and asked herself, *Why should I wonder about such a thing? I'm certainly not interested in a future with this man—or any other, for that matter. I've had it with romance! It almost got me killed.* She attributed her nonsensical thinking to the morphine and her extreme fatigue.

* * * * *

Andrew was in his last year of medical training before he would become a fully certified and licensed doctor. His mind was not yet made up as to what field of medicine to specialize in. His current training was in the area of surgery. But what field of surgery was yet to be determined. Neurosurgery was the option he was leaning toward. His thought was to do research and concentrate on this subject as part of his MD program. And now he had a perfect patient to complete this part of his study. She had a seemingly irremovable object in her head—a bullet fragment—and perhaps he could be the one to develop a surgical technique to remove it.

His mind kept going back to his bedside vigil with Carrie and the dream he had about walking hand in hand with her. *Impossible!* he told himself. *I could not ever have that type of a relation with Carrie. First of all, I don't think I could fall in love with or marry someone who is a cripple. Secondly, it is unprofessional, unethical and immoral for a doctor to get involved personally with a patient. No, my future with Carrie will be as her physician only.*

In time we may grow to be friends. But it will never be anything more than that.

He knew, however, that he may be fooling himself.

* * * * *

Carrie had a constant stream of visitors at her bedside while she recovered at Northwestern Hospital. Most of them were parents who came to thank her for saving their children. Lewis and Jennie came to see her and wanted to meet Dr. Peterson; however, he was not available at the time they were there, so they never got to meet him.

Occasionally, Carrie would drift into a deep sleep due to the effects of the medications she was taking and her weakness. Her visitors were told to wait until she awakened once more. Only two at a time were allowed in the room with her, and only for a few minutes.

On Saturday afternoon after the shooting, the Clay County Sheriff paid Carrie a visit. "Miss Wilson," he started out, "I need to ask you a question about the school shooting. The story that we have put together is self-explanatory, and you probably cannot add much more to it. The letters the shooter wrote, the eyewitnesses, and the injury and medical reports make this an open and shut case. There is only one question I need to ask you: Did you ever do anything that would have motivated this man to want to kill you?"

Carrie looked at him with a puzzled look on her face. "Nothing, Sheriff. Not a thing," she answered. "His behavior from the beginning was very troubling, and I saw early on that it would lead to a bad ending for both of us. In fact, I told him on several occasions that I wanted nothing more to do with him. I'm just glad that none of the children were hurt, other than some of them getting frostbitten."

"From the reports and from witnesses, it appears that Carrie Wilson was a hero," the sheriff smiled at her.

"Well, I'll take no credit or praise for what I may or may not have done. I just wish to give any glory to God for directing and protecting me through the entire ordeal."

"Well, I want to thank you, Miss Wilson," the sheriff said as he stood to leave. "You're one lucky woman."

Carrie's parents came on the train from their home in Massachusetts to visit her. For the benefit of Carrie they traveled together and were civil to each other—at least while they were with her. They stayed in a hotel in Fargo. Carrie didn't know if they stayed in the same room or if they got separate rooms. She never asked, although she wondered.

* * * * *

One afternoon, Andrew walked into Carrie's room pushing a wheelchair and carrying a pair of crutches. "Carrie, today you will be learning to become proficient using a wheelchair and maneuvering with crutches. It is a warm, sunny day, and I'm sure you'll enjoy getting out and breathing the fresh spring air. We'll make sure you are warm, since it is a little breezy out." Andrew reached for her to pick her up out of the bed and help her into the wheelchair.

"Doctor, I think we'd better let the nurses do this," Carrie quickly said. Carrie was very surprised at what he was attempting to do, since it was usually the nurses who accomplished that chore. The attending nurse walked in as Carrie was voicing her protest and was surprised that the doctor had not summoned her for the transfer. She got another nurse, and they transferred Carrie to the wheelchair.

As Andrew and the nurse pushed Carrie down the hall, she thought about how inappropriate it was for the doctor to try handling her. *Maybe I should request a new doctor,* she thought to herself.

They went outside to the courtyard with Andrew pushing Carrie for several minutes. Then he stopped and walked around to the front of her. "It's your turn to wheel yourself," he said.

Carrie was hesitant at first but then begin to wheel the chair using her strong, but very shaky, arms. After a short time, she stopped. "I am still a little weak, Doctor," Carrie responded in a tired voice.

"Let's rest here, Carrie," the doctor suggested as he pushed the wheelchair alongside a bench where he sat down beside her.

The doctor and patient talked at length about the medications Carrie was taking and how long she would be taking them. The conversation then turned to the bullet fragment still lodged in her head. Andrew explained why it was so difficult to remove.

During a lull in the conversation, Carrie wanted to turn their discussion to a previous subject. "Dr. Peterson let me show you what I wrote about my dream. Let me first tell you something. I am able to recall almost all of my dreams the morning after. It is an unusual talent I have . . . and have had ever since I was a little girl."

Andrew remained rather skeptical and replied in a manner that expressed his doubt on the subject. "You really place a lot of stock into your dreams, don't you? So what did you dream about?"

Carrie suddenly had second thoughts about telling her doctor. *Why tell him if he has no belief or faith in what I want to tell him?* she asked herself.

"On second thought, I think I'll just keep it a secret," Carrie said quietly. "I think you'll only make fun of it. But someday you'll believe me . . . mark my words." Carrie folded the piece of white paper and placed it back in the pocket of her hospital gown.

"You really believe this happened," Andrew questioned, "and it's not just a dream in your mind?"

Carrie looked at the handsome young medical student and confirmed her earlier conclusion: she and the doctor would probably not be compatible with each other in any personal relationship, contrary to what she had been told in her dream. "My dream happened just as surely as you and I are sitting here," the young teacher answered. "I guess you're not a believer in dreams, are you, Doctor?"

"I guess not," he answered in a subdued manner. "I only believe what I can observe in the real world or under a microscope. It would be nice if we doctors could close our eyes and magically dream what treatment or medicine we should use on our patients."

At that point the doctor stood up and began to push Carrie back to her room. Neither of them spoke. Andrew realized that what he had said to Carrie was unkind and he was sorry. It was destroying her hope, and she needed as much of that as she could get. He was about to say something to her, but he thought it be best to not say anything at all under the circumstances.

Before the nurses had placed Carrie comfortably into her bed, Andrew finally broke his silence with Carrie. "I wish I had your faith. Maybe someday." Even before Carrie had time to respond, he was on his way out of the door. He made the decision not to have contact with her apart from her medical requirements.

During Carrie's stay in the hospital, Andrew continued to order and encourage the use of the wheelchair for her. The nurses supervised this activity to make certain no mishaps occurred with the wheelchair. On nice days, this activity would be accomplished outside on the hospital grounds. When he was at the hospital, Andrew also took his turn in pushing her and letting her move herself by turning the wheels with her arms. He knew she needed to become proficient in using the wheelchair if she was going to continue her teaching career.

* * * * *

Carrie was lying in her hospital bed on a Tuesday morning when two of her doctors entered the room. They had invited Andrew to accompany them as they were about to tell Carrie some good news and some bad news. They all gathered around Carrie's bed and were about to start when Andrew interrupted, "How about if we set Carrie in the wheelchair so she's more comfortable." Carrie agreed. Two of the nurses helped her get situated.

Carrie was aware of the possibility that her injuries would have no lasting physical effects on her, except for her legs. There was no feeling in her left leg and very little in her right leg. She and Andrew had talked about this on a couple of occasions. It was not a pleasant thought for Carrie, but it needed to be addressed.

Doctor Ten Napel began the consultation. "Miss Wilson, we have good news for you. You may leave the hospital tomorrow morning. The bad news is, we need to inform you that the bullet lodged in your head is in a location where it is impossible to remove without the danger of causing more permanent physical impairment. Even worse, any attempt to remove the bullet may cause death. You may need to live the rest of your life with the bullet in your head. Also, we have been unable to determine what is causing your inability to walk or why you have no feeling in your legs. It is something that needs more study. The three of us are of the opinion that it may have something to do with the sciatic nerve."

"What is the sciatic nerve?" Carrie asked.

Andrew took over the discussion. "The sciatic nerve is the longest nerve in the body, traveling down from both sides of the spine and along the back of the legs to the feet. This nerve can affect motor movement of the leg muscles, so any damage to it can cause leg muscle pain. If the nerve is pinched enough or damaged, it can cause you to become crippled, which could be what happened."

Carrie sat in silence for a few moments. She knew practically nothing about sciatic nerve or its effect on the body. All she knew was she could not walk. "So, my being crippled is caused by a nerve?" Carrie asked.

The room was quiet for another moment. Everyone in the room knew this meant she could be in a wheelchair for the rest of her life. Andrew finally gave Carrie a definitive answer. "We are not completely sure what it is. It is very possible that some nerves are being affected, but exactly which ones and why are the big questions. It is possible that someday, new and improved medical procedures will be developed to correct your condition. This is one of the areas I will be researching in my work."

Andrew walked over to Carrie in the wheelchair and placed his hand on her shoulder. Tears began to appear in her eyes as she was thinking about being crippled the rest of her life. The full consequences of this tragic event in her life were now beginning to become more real than just a bad dream.

The other doctors immediately realized that their role in this consultation was no longer needed and that their younger medical colleague could handle it. Their opinion of Andrew Peterson was that he was young, but he was a master surgeon. He was also a caring person.

After the other two doctors had left the room, Carrie looked at Andrew and questioned, "This is the first I have cried since just after the shooting. Why is that?"

"Only you can answer that question, Carrie," Andrew responded. "Maybe up until now you haven't thought about the full consequences of the shooting. Your mind has been occupied with getting well. Maybe up to now you have had your mind fixed on the fact that certain circumstances saved your life."

"What circumstances are you talking about?" she asked.

"Oh, the poor aim of the shooter, your ability to outrun him, the fact that he ran out of bullets, the township people coming to your aid, and a host of other factors and timing."

Carrie looked into Andrew's eyes and then closed her eyes in disgust. Andrew noticed her facial expression and asked, "What are you thinking, Carrie? Your expression indicates you strongly disagree with me."

"You give absolutely no credit to God for protecting me, and I give *all* of the credit to Him. Maybe that's the difference between us in our faiths. You would credit the miracle that happened at the Spring Prairie school that morning to random chance. I give all the credit to God."

Andrew did not appreciate Carrie's comment and became quiet. *What can I say to her?* he thought. *We all don't show our faith in the same way. She just doesn't know me, I guess.*

Carrie realized immediately that she had said some things that may have seemed unkind to him. She had to say something to mellow her words. "As I have been lying in this bed all these hours, I have been doing some soul searching. Since the shooting, I have begun to wonder why God has placed me in this position. . . the strange twist of events in my life. I have been suddenly placed in the position where my future seems to be in a dark tunnel. I just can't accept that this is God's will for the rest of my life."

Andrew sat, silently looking at her, waiting for her to continue. He wanted to say something, but he didn't know what he could say.

"Or maybe God just doesn't care," she said at last with a look of anger clouding her face. "Maybe I should just be angry. Maybe I will always be a cripple. Maybe I will be unable to continue my teaching career, and I sure don't want to go back to my mother's home back east. If there is a God, why did He allow this to happen to me?"

Andrew suddenly interrupted. "Carrie, don't say things like that. You are a beautiful, kind, resourceful, and friendly woman. You have a great future ahead of you. People will look inside of you and . . ."

"It's okay, Doctor," Carrie interrupted him. "I can't be angry with God for very long. Without Him, where would I be? And do you want to know something?" she added with a smile, "I will walk again—and soon. God protected me and I should not be disappointed. The fact is . . . I still trust Him and give any credit to Him."

Andrew began to realize that this woman—no matter the circumstances—would react in a positive manner. He thought, *If the universe had to choose one person to suddenly have an accident, become crippled, and still remain positive, Carrie would be the perfect candidate.*

"Let me pray," Carrie responded. She did not wait for Andrew's approval. "Lord, I want to thank You for Dr. Andrew and his help in removing the bullets from my body. Forgive me for ever thinking that You are to blame for the shooting. Help me to look at my future in a positive manner. Be with Dr. Andrew as he continues his medical studies. Soon, You will provide him with the medical knowledge to remove the bullet from my head so I will walk again. Amen."

Andrew kept his eyes closed for a moment. This little prayer session by Carrie made him feel uncomfortable, yet encouraged. He admired her, once again, for her devotion. He wondered if Carrie really meant what she had just prayed. He knew that the chances of her walking again were almost zero. But the fact was that he saw no neurological reason for her not being able to walk. The actual cause of her not having the use of her legs was a mystery to both him and the other doctors.

He said goodbye to her and left the room. He immediately went to where he was staying, packed his suitcase, and walked to the train depot. He had a train to catch. He had Carrie's prayer on his mind as he boarded the train for St. Paul. He began to wish he could have Carrie's spiritual understanding and attitude, but he did not. He vowed once again not to pursue any kind of romantic relationship with her, even though he might be tempted. Maybe they could just become close friends as he helped her in her recovery, but nothing more.

Chapter 4

March 22, 1913

*A*s the passenger train started its journey, reaching full speed on the outskirts of Moorhead, a thought entered Andrew's mind. *Carrie has capably demonstrated that she is able to maneuver her wheelchair and handle her crutches well enough so she can continue her career in teaching—that is if some school board will give her a chance.* Andrew needed to make sure that happened, and there was no better place for her to start that process than at the school where she had been teaching. The parents and school board would be helpful and sympathetic to her.

The only question was whether she would want to go back and teach in the school where the shooting had taken place. The trauma that she had been through might be too much for her to even want to revisit the area—let alone walk into the school-house. She may still have some bad memories or experience frightening flashbacks of the incident. She didn't seem to have any residual effects of being scared and seemed to talk openly about the tragedy, but revisiting the scene of the crime could have a detrimental effect on her. It was possible the incident could produce a delayed-trauma effect, although she displayed no outward sign of it at this time.

Many of the parents felt that their schoolchildren's lives had been saved that morning by the teacher leading the shooter out of the school and across the road so that the children could get away. They realized Carrie had drawn the man away from the children even though it meant placing her own life in danger. Andrew had talked to some of the parents who had visited Carrie in the hospital. Many of them affirmed that her living through that dreadful experience was a miracle.

There was one other problem. Teaching a class from a wheelchair in a city school was one thing, but teaching in a country school was quite another. With the snow in the winter, just getting herself into the building would be nearly impossible for Carrie. She would need to maneuver from her desk to the coat room to get coal for the stove. And with the toilet facilities being outside in the elements, Andrew wasn't sure how Carrie could possibly manage the task alone. *How can a person in a wheelchair overcome these obstacles and still concentrate on the task of teaching children?* He contemplated.

As the train was well on its way toward the Twin Cities, Andrew walked up the aisle to where the conductor was seated. "I have a favor to ask you. Could you let me off at the Stockwood depot, and I will catch the next train?"

The conductor looked at the doctor for a moment. "What on earth could you possibly want in Stockwood?" he asked. "There's nowhere for you to stay there, and I can't imagine why you would want to go there. No, this train is not stopping at Stockwood for you or anyone else." The conductor seemed slightly irritated.

"I'm a doctor and I have to see a patient a few miles from the depot," Andrew answered. His statement was somewhat true, although not completely.

"I don't care if you have to see the President of the United States," the ill-tempered conductor told him, "this train will *not* stop!"

"How about if I pay you another fare?" Andrew asked the portly man.

"I absolutely cannot do that. We are not scheduled to stop at that station today, and we are already behind schedule."

Andrew pleaded once more with the conductor, but with no result.

Andrew walked back to his seat. He wanted to visit the school where the incident happened and the place where Carrie stayed. He relaxed for a moment, closing his eyes and wondering what to do next. His mind wondered off to Carrie's life and the future that this unfortunate occurrence had stolen from her. He wanted to know more about her—her past, her interests, her hobbies, and the shooting. But he also knew that getting personally involved with a patient was unethical on many levels. Maybe he was making a big mistake by involving himself in her life, but something told him he should try.

Andrew's thoughts were interrupted by one of the brakemen coming through the car, "Hey, Max," he called out to the conductor, "we're going to slow down enough to catch a small bag of important mail. Get ready."

Andrew kept his eyes shut, pretending he did not hear what the brakeman said to the touchy conductor. *Here's my chance,* he said to himself. *I'll just jump off when the train slows down.* He quickly grabbed his suitcase and book satchel and walked to the opposite end of the car from where the conductor was sitting. He opened the railcar door and positioned himself on the steps leading down to the ground. The train began to slow. Andrew knew that the train would not stop completely and he needed to guess when the most opportune time would be to jump. He closed his eyes and imagined when the train had slowed to a good jumping-off point. He opened his eyes and looked at the ground; he knew the engine was about to speed up again. His eyes searched frantically for a landing target in an open area where there was nothing that he would trip on and still allow for his forward movement. Suddenly, the train began to speed up. He quickly jumped clear of the train, hit the ground on his feet, and walked off next to the westbound tracks.

Inside the depot he saw the agent sitting at his desk. "How big is this town," Andrew asked him.

"Well, we have a bar, a hotel, a general store, an elevator, and this depot," the agent responded. "And there are about six houses with families."

"Which way is the Spring Prairie Township School?" Andrew inquired.

"Just walk down the westbound tracks, take the first road to the right, and go north three miles. It's on the west side of the road. But be careful . . . a woman teacher was recently shot there."

Andrew walked a short distance and found a bush thicket where he could safely hide his suitcase and book satchel. He needed to take a chance in hiding them because they were too heavy to carry the distance he needed to walk—at least three miles. There was no rain in sight, so his luggage and books would likely remain dry. Carrie had told him approximately where the school was where she had been shot.

Andrew had read that on the morning of the crime, the shooter had probably walked to the school from the Stockwood railway depot or from Glyndon. It must have been true because it wasn't long before Andrew saw what looked like a white schoolhouse in the distance on the west side of the road. Since it was Saturday, school would not be in session. Perhaps someone would be there doing some work on the building. Maybe the replacement teacher would be inside. Mostly, he was hoping the door would be unlocked so he could get warm—at least out of the chilly March north wind he was walking into.

He was in luck. A horse and wagon were parked in the driveway with some tools and lumber lying on the bed. *Apparently, someone is fixing up inside,* Andrew said to himself.

Andrew cautiously walked inside. A man and two boys were standing by the hanging portrait of George Washington. "Howdy," Andrew said.

The three men stood quietly for a few seconds looking somewhat afraid and distrustful. *The last time a stranger walked into the school, he shot the teacher,* they were all thinking.

"My name is Andrew Peterson . . . Dr. Andrew Peterson. I am one of Carrie Wilson's doctors. I was on my way to St. Paul where I am in my last years of medical training. I made a last-minute decision to come to this school to see where the teacher was shot. The news has spread far and wide concerning the miracle of the teacher being spared."

The three men continued to be skeptical and looked at each other. Andrew knew he needed to convince them that he was who he said.

The older man finally broke the silence. "My name is Ole Swenson. The two boys here are Fredrick and Theodore Larson. How is Miss Wilson?"

Andrew continued in his attempt to convince the disbelieving individuals. "Miss Wilson . . . Carrie . . . is healing. Her speech is improving steadily. All of the bullets in her body were removed except one. The bullet in her head cannot be removed . . . at least not at this time. The other doctors and I think it is maybe causing her to be crippled. The good news is that she is able to maneuver herself quite capably in a wheelchair. I saw her just this morning, and she prayed before I left her."

There was a sigh of relief from the three men. They obviously believed the doctor.

Fredrick decided he would take one more step in trusting the visitor. "We would like to take you to our farm where Miss Carrie was staying and has a room. You can have lunch with us." Theodore agreed. They knew their mother would welcome the stranger as an angel sent by the Lord.

"What are you fixing here?" Andrew inquired as he looked around.

Ole answered, "We are repairing some of the bullet holes in our nice school building that the gunman left behind. We are looking for more holes. One of them we won't be able to fix . . . the one in the blackboard. We can patch the one in the entryway and another one above the clock on the south wall. The man shot sixteen bullets. We found some of the casings in the snow."

"He must have been a poor shot," Andrew commented.

"Yes," Theodore replied, "and Thank God he was a poor shot! And that he had to reload his five-shot revolver three times.

Our teacher was smart and kept moving. She was fast and the man shooting at her was apparently slow and awkward."

It wasn't long before the wagon was back at the Larson farm. Lewis, the boys' father, greeted the doctor with the same skepticism that Andrew had encountered at the school. Finally, Lewis blurted out the truth. "You can surely understand why we may not trust someone who all of a sudden shows up at our school. That's exactly what happened the morning Carrie was shot. We were unaware of her past relationship with that fellow and that she needed protection." Lewis was still not fully convinced about their surprise visitor. Both Lewis and Jennie had visited Carrie in the hospital, but they had never met any of her doctors. They needed to find out more about him.

"Tell us about you, Doctor," Jennie asked as they sat down at the table and she handed him a cup of egg coffee.

Sensing that his hosts still questioned the authenticity of his story and the purpose for the visit, he explained, "Let me tell you first the reason I am here. I am one of three doctors working with Carrie Wilson. All of the bullets have been removed from her body, except one—the one in her head. It is in a place where we are afraid to even attempt to touch it. Removing it could possibly cause further damage. That's the best case scenario. Of greater concern is that it could cause her death. The bullet apparently damaged a nerve which is causing her the inability to walk. At least that's the only plausible theory our medical team can formulate at this time.

"I'm going to be very honest with you. I have gotten to know Carrie quite well in the past two weeks, and I have become very interested in her case. It is my professional opinion that Carrie needs to return to teaching as soon as possible. It would be healthy for her and would do her spirit good. She is very strong in her arms and would have no trouble maneuvering her wheelchair around the classroom. You may need to move the outhouse closer to the schoolhouse door to aid her in that detail. She will need occasional assistance in maneuvering through the elements at various times of the year, of course. But I am sure that one or more of the boys and girls would be more than willing to help her."

"What about her head?" Lewis asked. "Might the bullet shake loose as she moves her head or turns over in bed on her pillow?"

"At this point that's unlikely. The bullet actually broke into two pieces as it entered her head. One of the pieces I was able to remove. It was just under the skin. The other piece is actually lodged in her tissue. It is close to a nerve which my colleagues think is the cause of her inability to walk. However, I have my reservations about that theory. I think there may be something else that is causing her paralysis."

"What else could it be?" Jennie asked.

"I'm not at liberty to say now as it is only speculation on my part."

Another of Lewis and Jennie's son's, Norman, came rushing into the house with the urgent news, "Molly is by the barn and won't get up. She's sick and lying on her side with a bellyache, I think."

Lewis quickly turned his attention from Andrew to the best workhorse that the Larson's owned. Lewis and Andrew jumped up from the table and headed for the door, with Lewis out in front.

Molly had been pulling a sled for the better part of two days hauling logs from a grove of felled trees at the Sauer farm across the road. She was lying on her side by the barn with her stomach bloated and distended. Andrew was the first to suggest a cause. "She's been eating too much of something . . . she has gas trapped in her stomach." Turning to Lewis he asked, "Do you have any idea what she may have been eating?"

Lewis was surprised at the quick analysis from his guest. "Oats, hay, and water . . . that's all," he answered. "Maybe she got too much. She hasn't had any green grass because there is none this time of year. But if we don't get the gas out of her stomach, she'll die. I know this because we had a horse five years ago that died from the very same thing. I didn't know how to get the gas out of her stomach back then, and I still don't know what to do."

"Can she just throw up whatever she ate?" Lena asked.

"Horses cannot vomit," Andrew answered.

Andrew knelt beside the horse that had mothered three colts and two fillies. He gently rubbed her neck. "You're in pain, aren't you, girl?"

The gathered family members watched as the young doctor touched the horse with his large tender hands, while trying to think of what he could do to relieve the pain in this valuable animal. Even the family members involved with farm and household chores stopped what they were doing and came to see about the ailing horse. Andrew turned to his audience, which had by this time grown to include all of the Larson family. "We need to get the gas out as soon as possible. If you will allow me to perform a procedure that will bring her quick relief, she will at least have a chance of survival. Don't worry . . . prior to entering medical training, I worked for a vet for a couple of summers."

Lewis stood with his back to the brisk March wind, still questioning in his mind whether or not the man next to him was a real doctor. Finally, he said to the young man, "Okay, Doc . . . what can we do? Try your best to save Molly. We will help."

Andrew looked at the young farm boys and said, "I'll need a quarter-inch steel rod and a fire to get it hot. I need to sterilize it. We'll heat the rod on one end and then burn it through the stomach wall to let out the gas. The heat will cauterize the flesh. Molly should get relief immediately and we should be able to get her to stand up fairly fast. Whatever she ate is not only giving her gas, but also paralyzing her back end. She's unable to move her hind legs freely."

"Let's get it done," Lewis said. He was now convinced the young doctor knew what he was talking about and could capably do what he said he would.

Soon Frederick and Theodore returned with a steel rod sticking out of bucket of hot coals from a fire that burned around the clock in the pump house stove. Andrew buried one end of the rod into the bucket of glowing hot coals and let it sit for about two minutes. "Now, I'll need a clean white cloth to wipe the ashes off of the hot end of the rod."

Lena stepped forward and offered her clean white apron. "It was put on clean this morning," she said helpfully.

Andrew then took the rod from the boys with the pair of leather gloves they had also brought and positioned the hot rod next to Molly's stomach. The sudden quick impact and incision piercing through the stomach wall caused a sizzling sound, followed by the whistling of gas coming from Molly's bloated stomach as the rod was pulled out. The beautiful horse didn't flinch a bit. The stench of burnt flesh stung the noses of the onlookers. The girls winced in reaction to the pain they imagined Molly felt. The doctor then pushed on the bloated stomach, forcing out more gas. Everyone watching could smell the stinky odor coming out and witnessed the almost immediate relief to Molly's body and spirit.

"Now we need to get her up and walking," Andrew announced, looking at the anxious Larson family. "We'll need two ropes to position around her back end and then we'll get on either side of Molly and pull her up. This is going to take a lot of strength. Her front legs will stretch out and then the back legs will follow."

"Boys," Lewis ordered, "get those two short ropes from the horse barn."

Meanwhile, Andrew knelt again by Molly's head and began stroking her tenderly. The big horse's demeanor seemed to be relaxed as her eyes fixed on the medical doctor turned veterinarian. Out of nowhere little Louise appeared on the other side of Molly's head and begins to stroke behind her ears.

The ropes were positioned under Molly's rear end with the men doing most of the lifting. The whole Larson family then got on either side of Molly and aided in lifting the heavy horse using the ropes. "Let's slowly move forward as well as upward and see if she'll stretch out her front legs," Andrew suggested.

To the surprise of the gathered family members, Molly slowly stretched out her legs. She was very patient and seemed to know what the doctor and the others were trying to do. Andrew wondered what he should do next. He had only heard about his neighbor doing this when he was a young boy on the farm. "You youngest children start rubbing Molly's back legs. Let's see if we can start the nerves and blood flow working again," the doctor said to his young help.

"Elmer, you continue to press Molly's stomach so that any of the remaining trapped gas will empty out." Molly was used to members of the Larson family rubbing her body in various places. Soon Molly was walking. Within ten minutes she was walking with ease and starting to run.

"We need to find out what she ate so she doesn't do this to herself again. Where was she yesterday or this morning?" Andrew inquired.

"She was across the road at the Sauer farm," Fredrick answered.

"Let's walk over there," Andrew suggested.

Upon inspection of the ground around where the old tree logs were piled, Andrew spotted some dried up mushrooms that had come through the mild winter. "Aha! There's the culprit!" Andrew shouted, "Mushrooms are the worst kind of food for horses. They're tasty but produce gas in their stomach."

Fredrick retrieved a shovel from the bed of the wagon and buried all of the mushrooms he could find.

* * * * *

Andrew stayed for afternoon dinner at the Larson farm. It was a typical meal for one of Jennie's guests—homemade brown bread, fried steak, potato fries, homemade cheese, and a fresh cake that Lena had baked earlier that same morning. Jennie's Swedish egg coffee was a big hit with the doctor.

Their conversation centered on how to convince the school board to permit Carrie to continue teaching at the Spring Prairie Township School. Lewis was on the school board, and he and Jennie would attempt to convince the others on the board to agree to the new arrangement.

After dinner Jennie asked her three youngest children if they would give Andrew a tour of the farm. Joe, Jennie Louise, and Roy were soon walking from one end of the Larson farm to the other. They excitedly showed him the livestock, the chicken coop, the machinery area, the pump house, the granary, and introduced him to each one of the dogs, cats, and horses. Louise did much of the talking, as she had given this same tour on many occasions.

The tour was almost complete when they passed by a small garden next to an open field. Andrew suddenly stopped, with the Larson children one by one following suit. He was looking at three gravestones in the middle of the area where last summer's flowers had bloomed and now were all dried up. "What's the story with the gravestones?" he asked.

The children quietly walked back to the flower garden. They all focused their eyes on the three names listed on the three nine-by-nine-by-thirty-inch granite stones.

Joseph Andreas – Born 9/13/1897, Died 7/16/1901
Jennie Louise – Born 10/03/1899, Died 9/15/1901
Roy Edward – Born 11/21/1900, Died 8/14/1901

The children were quiet while the doctor waited for some response. He quickly realized that the story behind the tombstones was a very unhappy one. Finally, little Louise explained, "This garden is a very special place. It is where our two brothers and sister are buried. We plant flowers every spring so that they will smell them. We never knew them, but we honor them and someday we will meet them in heaven."

Andrew had been a witness to many sad moments in his few years of medical practice without becoming emotionally affected. But he could barely hold back his tears as he stood looking at the gravestones. He had felt the grief and sadness of this story through the voice of Louise. Then he noticed something. The names on the gravestones were the same as the children in his presence. "The names of your brothers and sister here are the same as your names."

Roy responded, "That's right. Mom and Dad named us after them . . . so that they would have a legacy."

Andrew pursued his inquiry. "How did they die? They all died in 1901 and only one month apart . . . one in July, one in August, and one in September. Exactly one month apart."

Joe responded, "They died during the diphtheria epidemic of 1901. It was a terrible time for Mom and Dad. Many of our friends' families in the township lost brothers and sister, and many families throughout the county lost children."

"And moms and dads," Roy added.

At that point they all became quiet once more. Finally, little Louise folded her hands and began to pray, "Jesus, be with the first Joe and Roy and Louise. Help us to remember them. And be with Mom and Dad as they still think of this terrible time. Help our teacher to get well in the hospital. And finally, thank you for sending us Dr. Andrew to save Molly from dying. Amen."

Andrew was not a praying man, but he suddenly realized that these three children were part of a very blessed family. He knew he wanted to get to know them better.

The tour disbanded with the boys walking toward the barn to work with the cattle, Louise walking to the chicken coop to gather eggs, and Andrew walking back into the Larson home. He saw mother Jennie standing by the sink washing dishes. He walked up to her and took her wet soapy hand. "Mrs. Larson, I just saw your children's grave markers in the flower garden. I want to give you my belated sympathy for your losses. That had to have been very hard."

Jennie wiped her hands with a towel, took a deep breath, and looked out the kitchen window. She answered the doctor, "Some of us had to be quarantined. Most of the family slept in the machine shed or pump house. Thank goodness it was summer. Had it been in the fall, winter, or spring, there would have been no school. The church was empty for almost four months. Many people actually stayed in the church."

"I remember when the outbreak occurred," the doctor responded. "The epidemic was worldwide. We studied it during my first year of medical school." Andrew placed Jennie's hand back into the sink and wiped off his soapy hand with a towel.

Lewis and Jennie invited Dr. Andrew out to the picnic table for a cup of herb tea. "This is the same tea we gave Carrie when she was lying on the couch waiting for the ambulance to come," Jennie said. "Who knows . . . maybe it saved her life."

The doctor never waited for either of his hosts to initiate any conversation. "Tell me . . . how did you two meet? A Norwegian and a Swede don't just naturally attract each other. Or do they?"

Lewis started the story. "We met when we were both employed at the Buffalo River Mansion, about six miles southeast of here. It was started by a wealthy couple from Vermont who were looking for a place to invest their money. They were on their way out west and became marooned at the Stockwood station in the 1880s when rail service to the west was halted by a flood in North Dakota."

At that point Lewis took a sip of his tea and Jennie continued the story. "The couple decided to explore the area. They found the Buffalo River nearby and swam for hours. There were snakes and turtles, but they were used to seeing these reptiles back in Vermont. It didn't faze them. This is what the wife told us, but I assume there was a certain amount of embellishment to her story."

Lewis continued, "The couple decided to latch on to this untouched prairie property. They stopped in Moorhead at the courthouse and negotiated the deed to two hundred acres of land. For the next two years they built a mansion of thirty-six rooms on the property next to the river. They next advertised in several publications back east for vacations in a paradise mansion . . . The Buffalo River Mansion. People would take the train to Stockwood, ride a horse and buggy over to the mansion, stay the night or for several days and go back home or continue to the west.

"Don't tell me," Andrew interrupted, "You both went to work for this enterprise probably at the same time."

"Yes," Jennie answered, "Exactly. I came from Sweden with my family and needed a job. An ad was in the paper I saw at the general store in Glyndon. I had been studying English back in Sweden in preparation for our move to America and was able to read the ad. It was an opening for someone to work in the house doing just what I do best, washing and folding the bedding, shining the crystal and silverware, cooking and serving meals, and other miscellaneous domestic duties. I worked six days a week, slept in a small room in the basement, and ate in the kitchen. My only condition to my employer was that I would have Sundays off. My family observed Sundays as a day of rest and worship."

"So, how did Lewis get involved?" Andrew asked.

"The day I came to Glyndon from Norway by myself," answered Lewis, "I read the same ad and applied for a job at the mansion. It happened to be the same day that Jennie applied for her job. We were scheduled to start work the next day. Since both of us were still learning English, we made an agreement with each other to speak nothing but English to each other. There were two reasons we did that. First of all, our employer said that the guests staying at the mansion would be from many different countries, would be attempting to also learn English, and needed to converse in English to make it easier for their trip to the West. Secondly, Jennie and I needed to communicate in a common language. That was English."

"So what work did you do at the mansion, Lewis?" Andrew asked.

"I was the groundskeeper. I planted trees, flowers, the garden, and worked in the horse barn."

"So what about romance between you two?" Andrew continued his inquiry. "Something magical must have happened between you two."

Jennie, smiling at Lewis, answered, "I believe we fell in love from the first day. I saw this handsome young man with Norwegian blue eyes, and he saw my Swedish blue eyes. We both missed our homelands and needed comfort and friendship. When my Lindahl family found out that their Swedish daughter had met and fallen in love with a Norwegian young man, I believe they thought the world was coming to an end!

"We were very busy during our employment at the mansion. It was fun working and meeting all the people. Many times we were asked to accompany the children of the guests down to the Buffalo River to swim. Both Lewis and I learned to swim so we could save anyone who got into trouble in the water."

Andrew still did not have the answer to his main question. "So tell me about the romance. When did the first kiss happen? I assume the Norwegians and Swedes kiss occasionally . . . or do you just rub noses?"

Lewis and Jennie laughed and looked at each other. Lewis finally spoke up, "It happened one night when we were invited to dine with a family and their guests from Bulgaria. We served the guests and sat down with them to eat. They had brought their own booze with them from Bulgaria and became a little tipsy as the night wore on. There were three couples at the big oak table, and they each started demonstrating their kissing techniques. They soon turned to Jennie and me. Assuming we were married they said, "Show us how it's done in Minnesota."

"We had never even held hands up to that point," Jennie broke in, "let alone kissed! I was ever so embarrassed. However, Lewis boldly grabbed me and, from watching every one of the three couples kiss several times, smacked me right on my lips. They asked us to repeat the kiss. Applause followed, and soon after that the dinner party disbanded."

"Okay," Andrew nosed in further, "what happened next?"

Lewis fielded this question. "There was a big full moon that night, so I asked Jennie if she wanted to go for a walk. She did and that is when I asked her to marry me. That was on a Saturday. She accepted and we decided to go to church the next day and announce it to Jennie's parents and to the entire congregation, which was the custom. Jennie announced it in Swedish and I did it in Norwegian. By announcing it in church, our parents could not refuse to bless the proposed marriage.

"Our biggest wedding gift was from our employer. A beautiful bedroom set. It had been shipped to the mansion from back east. Boston, I believe."

"Well, that's a great story about love blooming in an unlikely place. I hope that happens to me someday," Andrew applauded. He then looked at his pocket watch and announced, "I'd better get on the road if I'm going to catch the last train going east out of Stockwood tonight."

Andrew stood up and shook the hands of his hosts. He had just met what he thought were among the nicest people he had ever known. He had also earned their confidence by saving the life of their best horse. More importantly, he started the ball rolling on the school board's rehiring of Carrie to teach again at the Spring Prairie Township School.

Before he left he checked on Molly, his equine patient. Little Louise walked with him to the barnyard. The horse was doing just fine.

"Thank you for making Molly well," Louise said graciously, "I thought she was going to die."

"You are most welcome, little Louise."

"You can just call me Louise," she answered, "I am starting to grow and it is my birthday at the end of next month. I will be eight years old."

Theodore gave Andrew a ride to the railroad depot at Stockwood. He picked up his suitcase and books from where he had hidden them and talked the depot agent into letting him gain access to the caboose of a freight train going to Minneapolis. It would be slower, since the passenger trains had the right of way, but by only by a few hours.

On the way to Minneapolis, he had several hours to think about what had taken place since he left the Twin Cities in early March. He was called in on an emergency shooting incident, became obsessed with a beautiful teacher patient, probably saved her life, jumped off a train, saved the life of a bloated horse, met a farm family that was the picture of a perfect family, and listened to a story of true romance on the prairie.

He thought about his own future in medicine—his own personal desire: to someday meet a beautiful woman, get married, and raise a family. Maybe Carrie was that person. He would return to Moorhead soon and could schedule an appointment with her. He knew this would present a professional conflict for him—getting personally involved with a patient he was treating. But he was already involved, having visited where she lived and met her host family.

Chapter 5

March 31, 1913

*B*y the end of March, the doctors had all but given up on the removal of the bullet fragment left in Carrie's head. Dr. Andrew Peterson had done everything that could be done. Every other bullet wound had healed beautifully, and she was in full recovery—except that she was still unable to walk. It was evident to Carrie's team of doctors that the bullet left in her head was affecting only the movement of her legs and not her memory, speech, thought processes, or other nervous systems. But Andrew remained skeptical of the theory that the bullet had rendered her crippled. He suspected some other reason—either medical or otherwise—was responsible for her inability to walk.

Carrie was released from the hospital on March 31. The doctors gave her orders not to do anything strenuous until about September. She went back to the Larson farm and was moved into a small room on the main floor since her being crippled made it nearly impossible for her to climb the stairway to the room she had occupied before the shooting. She was able to get around with a pair of crutches and her wheelchair. She began immediately to help Jennie with light chores around the house—washing dishes, making coffee, patching clothes, and keeping her eye on and entertaining the younger children. These were all activities that were not strenuous and had been approved by Andrew.

All Carrie needed to once again teach was to obtain the approval of the township school board. Many of the people within the township and county believed the teacher would not resume teaching at all; let alone teaching at the same country school. But Carrie loved teaching, and she loved the children in the country community. The Larsons were like a mother, father, and family to her. It was the "home" she had always longed for but never had. It was even better than the home where she stayed when she taught at the Amish school in Pennsylvania. *It is much better than my childhood home back in Massachusetts,* she often thought.

* * * * *

On the first of June, Carrie decided to travel to her child-hood home in Massachusetts to see her parents. They had vis-ited her in the hospital a few days after the shooting and stayed long enough to make certain that she was going to survive. Her mother and dad had been separated for a few years, but for the benefit of Carrie they had traveled on the train together to Moorhead soon after the shooting incident.

Her father bought and mailed to Carrie a roundtrip train ticket to Boston. Lewis and Jennie felt that it would be a little risky for her to travel alone, especially on a train; however, she had to prove that she could function even as a crippled person. *I need to prove that I can function independently . . . that I won't be a burden to anyone,* she challenged herself.

Lewis called Andrew and told him that Carrie would be passing through Minneapolis on her way to Boston. "Maybe you can meet her as she changes trains," Lewis suggested.

When she arrived at the depot in Minneapolis, Carrie wasn't exactly overjoyed to see her doctor. *Oh, great! Another doctor! As if it's not stressful enough to be on my way to see my mother . . . now this. I just want to be done with doctors!* Carrie complained to herself.

"Carrie, you look good in street clothes," Andrew commented with a broad smile as he handed her a hot cup of coffee.

"I guess this is the first time you've seen me in anything other than hospital clothes," she replied with a chuckle. They chatted about things other than her medical condition as Andrew helped her with her baggage and pushed the wheelchair. They had only a few minutes to talk.

When Carrie got on the second train, she thought about their meeting and realized how very different he was outside of the hospital. He was friendly and personable. He was genuinely interested in how she was getting along and what was going on in her life. Not only that, he had put his very busy schedule on hold just to come and spend a couple of minutes with her. *Maybe he's sweet on me,* she thought to herself as a smile crept across her face. But then she stopped herself. *NO!* she thought. *I can't let this happen. I'm not going to risk losing my life over something I can easily live without. I don't need romance, and I don't want the hassles of a relationship. After all, look where it got my parents. I need to stop him before this relationship goes any further. He is my doctor only. Period!*

In Minneapolis Carrie had been able to maneuver sufficiently up into the train with the help of Andrew and some kind passengers. She did have a slight problem changing trains in Chicago. The train coming in from St. Paul was late, which meant that she needed to wheel her chair to the next gate much faster than what she was able to do. She arrived just as the train was pulling out of the station. The conductor looked back from the last car and saw her, and he immediately pulled the cord which signaled the engineer to stop the train. In a few short moments the train had backed up permitting Carrie and her wheelchair to board the last car. The conductor let her stay in the last car all the way to the next stop instead of making her maneuver her way to the fourth car up from the rear.

There was only one problem. The car that she was sitting in was the train's club car. The conductor told her that this particular car would soon be filled with many young military personnel and college students coming from other connecting trains. He helped Carrie get seated at a table and had a cup of tea delivered to her. Sure enough, the car did fill up quickly with the young men. They immediately spotted the very pretty Carrie sitting in the middle of the car, alone. Some of them crowded around her, moving to the table she was sitting at, ordering their drinks, and talking to her.

"Where are you headed for?" one of them asked.

"Massachusetts," she answered.

"Can I buy you a drink?" another young fellow asked.

"No, thank you," she answered politely. This routine went on for the next twenty minutes with practically every young man in the car vying for her attention. She answered each politely. Carrie wanted to sleep for a while, and this routine was not going to permit it. She needed to do something. She reached for her crutches, which she had partially hidden under her seat and covered with her coat. "Excuse me," she announced, and with great effort rose up out of her seat. She then walked with even greater put-on effort to the women's restroom. As she walked, the assembly of young men became quiet. When she returned, all of the military personnel had moved to different seats. Problem solved.

* * * * *

At her family's lake home in Connecticut, Carrie was visited by her many childhood friends and their families. The most interesting visit was from the parents of Michael Jenkins, the old boyfriend who had gone crazy and tried to kill her. The parents felt terrible about the entire affair and even wanted to pay for some of her medical costs.

"What is your prognosis?" Mr. Jenkins asked.

Carrie thought for a moment and questioned if she should say much. However, she knew that another operation was yet to come, and it would be expensive. She had saved only a small amount from her teaching job. Carrie wanted to be friendly to them. "Well, my doctor thinks there is not much hope that I will walk again. But I know that I will, and I will even run again. Dr.

Peterson is working with a medical group that is doing research on head injuries. He is hopeful that he and his team will come up with some type of procedure." Carrie stopped there and looked out the window of her parents' lake home where she was staying.

"We feel very bad about what happened," Mrs. Jenkins said, "and we want to help you in any way possible. We will pay for that operation whenever it takes place. Please give us the name and address of your doctor, and tell him that we will be in contact with him."

Carrie could not imagine what such an operation would cost. She knew that just the hospital personnel assisting on such a major procedure would be very expensive. "I will give that information to you and inform Dr. Peterson," she answered. "And I thank you for your concern and kindness."

Carrie did feel sorry for Michael Jenkins and especially for his parents. He was gone, but his mother and father were forced to live with the guilt of not recognizing their son's illness and doing something about it. *I could hate them and be bitter towards them,* she thought to herself, *but that is not the Christian attitude I need to have. I will maintain a lifelong friendship with them in an attempt to ease their pain.*

Many of the people who came to visit Carrie during her visit in Boston had known the man who had shot sixteen bullets at her. It was surprising to Carrie to find out from them that many of them suspected him of having mental problems. *I wonder why my friends never warned me about him,* she contemplated. *Many times our friends are the last to tell us unhappy news or of potentially dangerous situations,* she answered herself. *But, then again, I may have not listened to them.*

Carrie did not know exactly what had happened to her own parents' marriage. She had some ideas based on what their relationship was like when she was living at home and things that had happened when she had come home from college. But her parents were happy to see her and seemed to enjoy spending time with her. No one talked about the separation.

Carrie's friends were also happy to see her. They had all been made aware of the tragedy in her life by reading the accounts in the national press. Carrie shared with them the details of God's miracle protection that had occurred in her life.

The wheelchair became somewhat of an obstacle during Carrie's visit. She tried her best to overcome every barrier to her freedom of movement by using her hands, arms, and crutches, but sometimes she still needed the help of her friends and family assisting her. She was determined to do as much as she could by herself. She had made up her mind that she was going to teach once again at the Spring Prairie Township School. This trip was to be the time when she would prove to herself—and to the board—that she could do it.

Carrie thought about discussing with her mother the incident where she had slapped her when she was a small child. There wasn't a day that Carrie didn't think about it. Carrie was still quite bitter about it and she was sure the horrible incident was on her mother's mind also. It needed to be resolved. But by the time she was ready to return to Minnesota, she had not mustered the courage to bring it up to her.

On the way back to Minnesota on the train, Carrie had a chance to think about many things. One of the things concerning her was Andrew and his coming to meet her in Minneapolis on the first leg of her trip. *Did I show him some friendliness?* she questioned of herself. *What were his intentions by coming to the depot?* This train of thought led to her thinking about her future. She knew she wanted to get married someday and have children, but the thought of being in another relationship with a man sickened her. All she could think about was being controlled and dominated and threatened. Could it ever be possible to have another relationship without getting hurt again? And what if she did get into a relationship again and it ended in separation like her parents'? Did they really enjoy being married but living in separate houses? All of these thoughts and questions caused her to fall asleep.

* * * * *

Andrew traveled to Europe by ship in June to study neurosurgery under several renowned physicians in three different cities. Andrew wrote to Carrie several times during his trip to tell her of exciting advances he had discovered. In one of the letters, he asked her if she would join him in Switzerland the second week of August where he was studying and attending medical conferences. He needed a date for an international meeting banquet. They would also do some sight-seeing, and, naturally, he would pay all of Carrie's expenses.

Carrie didn't believe it was proper for her to meet him without a chaperone since they were not married. She also wondered if Andrew had forgotten that she was not able to walk. Sight-seeing would be very difficult for her. But maybe he had some other travel arrangement for them.

Carrie wondered if the reason behind Andrew wanting her to come to Europe was because he wanted his medical associates to see her as the subject of his medical research. He never mentioned anything about that in his letters, and she never asked. She needed to tell him that she was not interested in a personal relationship with him—only a professional one. She debated if she should write a letter to him or if she should wait and do it in person. She finally decided to write him a return letter.

Andrew:

Thank you for the invitation to come to Switzerland in August. I must respectfully decline at this time. I believe it would be improper to do such a thing as I am a single woman and you are a single man. Also, I am in the process of getting ready for the school year. So far the school board has not granted me permission to teach, but neither have they hired or even interviewed any other teachers. I believe God has it under control.

I am still staying with the Larsons, my gracious family here in Spring Prairie. Maybe I will see you the next time you are in Clay County

Carrie.

* * * * *

Carrie spent her time on the Larson farm learning how to manage without being able to walk. She commented to mother Jennie that she was working harder without the use of her legs than if she had use of them. She was developing strong arms from forcing her wheelchair over the rough farmyard terrain. Freddie Larson had fitted the wheelchair with special tires to help her more easily traverse the property, but it was still a lot of hard work to get from one place to another.

Carrie helped out with the Larson's garden by weeding and watering using a small pitcher. Freddie would haul water from the windmill pump. When the vegetables were ready to be harvested, she peeled them and helped with canning. She was also able to help with the daily milking of the cows. By bedtime each night she was very tired and would fall asleep very quickly. The neighbors began thinking of her as the Larson's hired lady.

Carrie had mother Jennie help her continue the sewing hobby she had learned from the Amish back east. Her mother in Massachusetts sent her a trunk of fine fabrics and materials from the fabric stores. Carrie shared them with Jennie and the Larson girls. People in the township begin to notice all of the women of the Larson household and their fine dresses.

Sewing from a wheelchair and without the use of her feet was very difficult, but somehow Carrie managed with the help of little Louise moving the treadle. Freddie eventually added a steel rod to the treadle of the sewing machine so Carrie could sew without having to "borrow" anyone's feet or legs. Little Louise was observing and learning the fine art of sewing also. On her first day back at school, Carrie was planning to wear one of her own creations.

One of the activities Carrie had enjoyed prior to the school shooting, which she no longer was able to do, was dancing. She would sometimes imagine how she could dance in a wheelchair. *Someday I will once again dance,* she mused to herself. She and Andrew had talked about when they would attend dances in their youth, he in Iowa and she in Massachusetts. He still attended them at social functions connected with the medical school sometimes when he was in St. Paul.

When she thought about it, she could see Andrew someday marrying a beautiful nurse or even a woman doctor and dancing at their wedding. Many of the medical schools were beginning to admit women into their medical programs.

Andrew! Why am I wasting my time thinking about him! she admonished herself. *I have no interest in that man outside of healing from my injuries. But why is Andrew so interest in me?* she kept wondering.

* * * * *

Without Carrie's knowledge, Andrew's influence with the school board was sufficient to permit Carrie to be considered and approved to continue teaching in the fall of 1913. She knew she could do it, and the parents of the children had full confidence in her.

Carrie decided to wait until the first day of school to revisit the property. Lena Larson—who spent much time cleaning desks, windows, floors, and walls at the Spring Prairie Township School—invited Carrie to come with her the Saturday before school began. Carrie declined.

* * * * *

September 1913

The first day of school was a difficult one for Carrie. She arrived an hour early. Theodore Larson gave her a ride with Nelly pulling the buggy. The black palomino had not forgotten her friend, Carrie. Theodore would make a second trip from the farm bringing the other children from the Larson household.

Theodore was one of the young men in the township who had his eye on Carrie. Since the day she arrived on the train in the spring of 1912 from the East Coast to interview for the teaching position, he was captivated by her. It made no difference to him if she was now crippled. He was aware of her every move around the farm. Of course, Carrie knew this right from the start. It didn't take her very long to realize that his interest in her was of a protective nature more than any romantic relationship. She knew if anything or any person threatened her, Theodore would be right there and have them for his breakfast.

There were other fellows, young and old, who would look for her whenever there was a township gathering of any sort. Theirs was more of an admiration-from-afar interest for which their attentive wives would sometimes physically turn their husbands' heads. The entire township had never seen a more beautiful woman. Now she was crippled. This aspect gave the men and boys a chance to come to her aid whenever she needed a lift up, a push along, or help getting down.

But despite Carrie's desire to get married and raise a family, the thought of romance was still an unwelcomed one. Ever since she broke up with Mr. Jenkins, she had very little interest in dating. She wondered what it would take to cause some romance to come back into her life once again. She wasn't even interested in her handsome doctor. She hadn't informed him of this fact, although he probably suspected it. *Maybe I will soon get a chance,* she often thought.

On her first day back teaching, Carrie was let off in front of the school. Teddy helped her out of the buggy and into the wheelchair. Carrie peered toward the open front door of the school. She looked down at the ground and could see where her former boyfriend had shot himself and died. In her mind she could still see his blood covering the dirt. The men of the township had built a wheelchair ramp so that Carrie could more easily gain access to the school. Just inside the door she could see where she had deflected the first shot that morning. On the wall next to the door molding, Carrie fingered the patched hole where the sheriff told her he dug out that first bullet, the one that had pierced her ear. Carrie felt a little faint as she closed her eyes and recalled the morning of March 5th. It was not a pleasant memory. Andrew had suggested that in order for her to gain closure on the dreadful event, she should revisit the entire path that she ran that morning. Otherwise, the bad memories of the event may accumulate in her mind and have a long-lasting effect on her mental and physical health. Carrie followed his advice and retraced her steps. Andrew was correct—she was able to gain closure from this part of the incident.

She continued inside the schoolhouse. She noticed the bullet hole in the slate blackboard that could not be repaired. She looked around the room and recalled the frightened faces of the children. She remembered sitting in front of the stove and sobbing as the first people showed up to help her. Her eyes started to well with tears again at the vivid memories.

Carrie wheeled herself out of the schoolhouse and back down the ramp. With great difficulty she wheeled herself up the driveway to the road and over to the Zion Lutheran Church. Carrie moved around the horse barn, the churchyard, and around the trees where she had tried to protect herself that horrifying morning. It was a clear reminder of how close she had been to death. Finally, she tried the front door of the church. This time it was open.

Taking her crutches from the back of her wheelchair, Carrie walked into the church. She knew what she had to do. Walking to the front, she managed to kneel at the altar and began to pray, *"Lord, as I retrace the steps I took on March 5th, I now realize that You and a host of Your angels were with me that morning. Thank You for this protection. It tells me that You have more work for me to do on this earth. Bless this day and the children that I will teach. Help me to instill in their minds that which will glorify You and be helpful to them this day and in the future. And please, Lord, grant me the ability to walk again one of these days. Amen."*

Within the hour Carrie was finally once again teaching in the Spring Prairie Township School—this time from a wheelchair. It would have its difficulties and inconveniences, but with the help of the older boys and girls she would managed. She welcomed each of the regular students as they arrived. She also met three new children as their parents brought them to school. There were some changes in the school. One was where the girls' toilet was located. It was close to the front of the school. This was for Carrie's ease and comfort.

Miss Wilson used the same opening exercise routine as she had on March 5th. The one change she was planning to make was to let some of her better readers read the Scripture lesson on certain days. Carrie would always pray.

One of the challenges that presented itself on the first day brought the class together in a cooperative effort. During the lunch recess when all of the students were outside playing, Carrie noticed some disturbing sounds in the wall behind George Washington's framed picture. Carrie knew immediately what the source of the sound was. Rats! Rats were in the wall! Carrie envisioned a mommy and daddy rat building a nest for the winter and making a cozy little home for their future family. *We need to get rid of them before they multiply,* Carrie said to herself. *But how can that be accomplished?*

Since Carrie's maneuverability in a wheelchair was not the best for killing rodents, she needed to enlist the older boys and girls to help out. When they came in from lunch recess and were seated, she spoke in a soft tone to them. "Children, we have a problem. Behind our first President there exists a family—or potential family—of rodents. Rats in particular. I need you to help me annihilate them—kill them, for you who haven't heard that word before."

Everyone turned their eyes toward George Washington and listened. The rats were still at it, whatever they were doing. All of the children quickly sat up straight. Some of the girls instinctively lifted their feet.

"Do we have any suggestions on how to get rid of these disease carriers?" the teacher asked. There were a host of suggestions. Jack Monson suggested that the wall be knocked down. Freddie Larson wanted to use some rat poison. Julius Mieffski said that he should stay the night with a flashlight and a broom and kill them one at a time when they started to race around the floor. There were other suggestions. The one that was most reasonable was voiced by Roy Larson. "Let's place pails of water on the floor, melt some animal fat on the top and leave them overnight. When we are not around, the rats will come out of the walls, smell the fat, jump onto the hardened coat of fat, and fall into the water and drown." Everyone applauded his suggestion.

Freddie and Roy Larson drove the horse and buggy back to the farm, fetched five empty pails, and got some animal fat that mother Jennie was saving to make soap. On their return they set the traps in motion. The five empty pails were filled with water from the spring close to the school and placed at various locations within the room. No bait was needed since the melted fat would lure them to the pails. The fat was melted outside and poured onto the pails of water. The smell permeated the entire room.

Everyone went home that afternoon wondering if the traps would work. When the children told their parents about the rats and the traps, they had their doubts. They were well aware of the threat the rats presented to the farmers, both health-wise and financially.

Everybody came to the school the next day anticipating an expected catch in the rudimentary traps. Were the rats too dumb as to get caught in such a simple trap?

When the class arrived they had a surprise. Two dead, drowned rats were in one of the pails. Many of the children wondered how the rats could be so stupid as to jump in—maybe even together. All day long the class carefully listened for more sounds in the wall but heard nothing. They thought that if any babies were in the nest, their demise would be next.

* * * * *

Andrew was living in St. Paul, Minnesota where he began a year of intensive medical research in surgery. He joined a group of medical doctors specializing in head injuries and the surgeries connected with them. He told the doctors that his goal was to develop techniques and instruments to remove foreign objects from the head. The doctors took an interest in the goal of their new younger partner. They did tell him that a great portion of his patients probably would not make it through their surgery since the injury and trauma would oftentimes be so severe that it would be beyond recovery. He also was aware of the many gangster-related encounters that would necessitate the use of his services, especially at that time in the cities of St. Paul and Minneapolis.

Carrie got occasional letters from Andrew telling her of the work he was doing. She wished he would stop writing, although the things he wrote about were interesting and usually were related to her medical condition.

About the first of October, Andrew wrote a letter to Carrie at the Larson farm. After the first letter, he waited for a reply—nothing. He wondered if maybe the letter did not arrive. He then wrote to Lewis Larson asking him to let him know of any noticeable change in Carrie's condition. He also added: "My research primarily deals with problems associated with head injuries. Many times these injuries do not have noticeable effects until months or even years later. We are working on new procedures and can see Carrie as a potential surgical candidate, should she ever need to have the fragment removed. As of now, however, we'd best leave well enough alone."

Two weeks later Andrew received a letter from Carrie.

Andrew:

Thank you for writing. I am sorry I did not answer your letter sooner. I was very busy at school with the children. Teaching was much easier when I could walk. I pray every day for you and that someone in your research group will find a way to permit the removal of the fragment from my head and that I will be able to walk again.

I know it is His plan for me, and I know that you will be involved.

Concerning a related matter, I would prefer that you not write to me on a personal level as I believe that you will someday want to marry someone better suited to your socio-economic level. I know I can never be that person. You are a kind and considerate person and doctor. I am certain God has a wonderful woman for you to spend your life with.

God bless you,
    Carrie Wilson

About a month later, Andrew notified the hospital in Moorhead that they needed to schedule an appointment with Carrie to take x-rays and review her injuries. It had been eight months since the shooting. "Please schedule another doctor to be with me as I examine Miss Wilson," the appointment request stated.

He wrote to Carrie and informed her of the upcoming medical appointment. At the end of his letter he added, "I trust you are feeling well and are happy in your teaching work. It is important to your recovery and health. I really miss all of our talks that we had when you were in the hospital. Maybe we can do that again on the farm sometime when I visit there." Carrie took from that last sentence that Andrew missed her and still wanted to have a relationship with her. Carrie was frustrated by Andrew's letter. Her letter to him stating that she was not interested in a personal relationship with him didn't seem to help.

The medical appointment was scheduled for November 10, 1913, at Northwestern Hospital in Moorhead. Andrew came in by train from Minneapolis on the 9th and stayed overnight at the Moorhead Hotel. The next morning he stopped by the hospital business office and asked about the bills that had piled up related to Carrie's hospital costs and care following the shooting. They were significant. Andrew needed to do something to satisfy the hospital with some payment. He knew what country schoolteachers were paid, and it would take her several years to earn enough to cover her personal expenses plus be able to pay down her medical bills.

The examination and consultation went well. Andrew acted in a professional manner when speaking to Carrie. The other doctors and nurses sensed that there was a deeper personal connection between the two, although more on the part of Andrew than Carrie. They had also heard rumors of a suspected romance between these two. Under normal circumstances Andrew would be asked about a personal relationship with a patient and pressured into ceasing it. But Doctor Andrew Peterson was a very in-demand surgeon, and any discussion on the subject was avoided.

"Miss Wilson, one of the things you will need to do is to exercise your legs. You should rub them several times a day to keep the muscles strong and attempt to get some feeling back to them. Otherwise, they will eventually become shrunken and completely useless."

Carrie looked at the assembled medical staff in a puzzled manner. "Do I just rub the muscles?" she asked.

"Rub both your legs and your feet . . . even the toes. Here, let me show you." Andrew knelt next to Carrie's wheelchair and placed both hands gently on Carrie's left shin and massaged it. He was expecting her to stop him based on her previous reactions. "Can you feel anything?" he asked.

"Not really," she answered.

"Well, your shin can feel it," the doctor responded, "and if it could talk it would tell you."

Carrie smiled. "So what else would it say if it could talk?"

"Well, let me ask it." Andrew positioned his right ear close to Carrie's knee and listened for a few seconds. "Both of them talked. One said, 'Keep doing that.' The other one said, 'Me too.' They both want to be rubbed regularly. Maybe you can get the Larson girls to help you rub them periodically. But I would not ask the Larson boys to do that, if I were you," he added with a smile.

Carrie returned his smile.

Andrew asked a few more questions and then checked her blood pressure, pulse, and reflexes. He made a few notes in Carrie's file. At that point the medical exam was over, and the other doctors and nurses left the room.

Carrie took a deep breath and asked, "Andrew, when do you think you can take the bullet out of my head?"

The doctor looked at Carrie with surprise. "That's a tough question to answer. I wish I had an answer for you. My best answer? At this time we should leave well enough alone."

Carrie looked at Andrew for a moment and spoke in a prophetic manner. "Doctor Andrew . . . you will soon operate on my head, you will remove the bullet fragment, and I will walk again!"

Andrew stood up and took a few steps back from the wheelchair Carrie was sitting in. He looked hard at Carrie, but he had no idea how to respond to what she just said—not in a way that wouldn't disappoint her, anyway. "How do you know that?" he finally asked.

Carrie looked straight at him and said confidently and clearly, "Because Jesus told me in the dream I had."

Andrew suddenly realized that this young woman either had a direct connection to the Almighty or was delusional. Now what was he going to say to the woman he would like to get to know better and maybe court? "When did Jesus tell you this?" Andrew asked.

"In the dream I had when I was unconscious in the hospital—after you operated on me. You have never read what I wrote about my dream."

"No, I haven't," Andrew affirmed.

"Would you like me to read it? I carry it in my purse. It is His promise to me. Here, you can read it," Carrie said handing the much worn note to Andrew.

Andrew quietly read the note two times. "You really dreamed this?"

"Yes, I did. And it will happen. Someday," Carrie said in a convincing tone.

"Carrie," the doctor began, "I am going to be perfectly honest with you. I will not operate on a delicate part of the human body because of a dream. It's just too risky. In addition, the hospital board may fire me and report me to the authorities if I ever did."

"Well, then, I will find a doctor who *will* operate!"

Andrew couldn't believe what he was hearing from Carrie. They were the words of a woman who was apparently running out of patience. She was becoming desperate.

What can I say to her? He thought to himself. *If I say anything, I will make her even more irrational.* Finally, Andrew sat down on a chair, folded his arms in front of him and said, "If you feel that way, I'll put you in contact with some of the surgeons I know who may consider performing the operation. I need to emphasis the word *may.* Meanwhile, I'll continue working on research to someday successfully perform the fragment removal. You're not the only person in this situation, you know. If you don't have it removed by some other doctor by the time I perfect a procedure, I will perform the operation for you. How does that sound?"

"That sounds good, Doctor Andrew," Carrie said agreeably.

Andrew stood up and left the room. He realized that the good feelings between him and Carrie had suddenly taken a twist in the road. This occurrence was something many doctors faced when working with patients who have conditions that are not easily cured. It had happened to Andrew a couple times previously, but not with a good friend. As he was walking down the hall, he realized that the reasoning and the warning of his associates not to get too involved with a patient was correct.

Before he left the hospital, he wrote two referrals for Carrie to two doctors, one in Omaha and one in Indianapolis. Andrew was not sure if she would go through with it. Most likely neither of the two doctors would want to travel to Moorhead to see Carrie. It was a long shot, but Carrie needed something to give her some hope.

* * * * *

Andrew kept in contact with Lewis Larson and told him of his research in head surgery. Occasionally, Carrie would see the letter as it arrived in the mail or would overhear Lewis mentioning the contents of the letter to Jennie. Both of the Larson parents liked Andrew ever since the incident with Molly, their best workhorse. They also were of the opinion that Carrie couldn't find a more suitable man to marry than Andrew. It was quite evident to both Jennie and Lewis that Andrew wanted the relationship to be headed that way. They sometimes would discuss just how a marriage like that would work, whether or not she could have children, how she would take care of them, and other aspects of raising a family while being crippled.

"I don't think Carrie feels for Andrew the same way Andrew feels for Carrie," Jennie commented. "Maybe that will change in the next few months."

"I don't think the doctor is telling us all he knows about Carrie's situation," Lewis said.

"What do you mean?" Jennie responded.

"I don't know what it is," Lewis answered. "I feel that Andrew knows more than he is telling Carrie or anyone else. In fact, I think he may be still trying to figure it out himself."

In the next letter he wrote to Lewis, Andrew mentioned the hospital bill. "I suggest you organize a fund-raising event at the school where people can donate money to offset some of these costs. It is very probable that Carrie will need further medical care—even further surgery—in the near future. Enclosed is a check for $50.00 to start the fund. In addition, I have asked the Hospital business office to cancel my fees. Please do not tell Carrie about this."

* * * * *

Carrie found herself thinking about Andrew often and was fascinated by the thought of him. He was handsome, smart, and had a great future in front of him. He would make a wonderful husband for some lucky woman. Carrie knew in her heart of hearts that she could be that woman—if only she would allow herself to be. But Carrie was afraid of getting into another relationship with any man. She knew that not all men were like Michael Jenkins. In fact, she believed only a very small percentage of the population possessed the mental instability and psychological problems that Michael had. Carrie had been terribly disappointed in her last relationship and she didn't want to inflict that same disappointment on anyone. Because she was now confined to a wheelchair, Carrie knew she could not be the kind of wife and mother from a wheelchair that she could if she had the use of her legs. She had become so self-conscious about her limitations and how they could potentially destroy a relationship that she was ready to abandon her dream of marriage and a family.

Whenever Carrie contemplated her condition and her future as a cripple, she panicked at the thought of never realizing her dreams. She soon came to realize that the best way to avoid panic and despair was to work. Hard and long. Carrie poured herself into her role as teacher, both at the schoolhouse and at the Larson farm, and took on every project she could find. The busier she was, the less time she had to dwell on her situation.

One day about two weeks after Andrew had written a personal letter to Carrie, he received a letter back. The letter contained his unopened letter and a brief written note from her. "Please do not send me anymore letters. I am not interested in any personal relationship at this time as I am very busy with other things right now."

This is the trouble with getting involved personally with a patient, he thought to himself. *My associates warned me about this.* Andrew was disappointed and a little puzzled. He had no idea why she had all of a sudden become cold toward him. He was beginning to wonder if the bullet lodged in her head had moved and was affecting her thinking or her emotional makeup. *Maybe it's even a delayed mental reaction,* he thought to himself.

However, he was encouraged by her words, "at this time." *Patience is the answer,* he reassured himself.

In the letter he had sent to her, he described a procedure that indicated a major advancement in the field of head surgery, as reported in the *Medicine Monthly*. Andrew thought Carrie should be aware of this medical breakthrough. He had sent a copy of the same information to Lewis for his information.

Both Lewis and Jennie noticed there was a rift between this couple and that something must have happened at their medical appointment. Jennie saw Carrie's unopened letter on her bed as she placed other mail there. Jennie shared her thoughts and concerns with Lewis.

At his next conversation with Carrie, Lewis read to her about the breakthrough in the surgical procedure. Carrie seemed quite interested, by the look on her face. She was trying to show her non-interest but listened closely.

Andrew placed the unopened letter and Carrie's reply in a drawer. He decided to forget about his pursuit of Carrie's heart and love and just concentrate on his studies and medical practice.

* * * * *

Summer 1914

Carrie continued staying at the Larson's and helping around the farm. During the summer of 1914 she had enrolled in classes at a college in Moorhead. She also took a couple of correspondence classes from a college back in Massachusetts. She attended regular church services and taught English classes to the parents of her immigrant schoolchildren.

There were also the two sons of Lewis Larson who were obviously "sweet" on Carrie. Neither of them had attempted to date her. Carrie and mother Jennie were able to notice the looks that the two boys gave her. Lewis, for some reason, was oblivious to what was going on. Freddie Larson did notice that there was not any interest in romance on Carrie's part. This he deduced from his conversations with her. He suspected that some emotional block was involved.

In the middle of August, Carrie wrote to the two referral doctors that Andrew had provided to her. Within a week a Dr.

Wheeler from Omaha contacted Carrie and told her that he would be on vacation in Fargo in a week and could visit with her.

A week later they met in Moorhead, and Dr. Wheeler examined the bullet wound in Carrie's head. He cut into the wound just slightly to explore where the lead fragment was situated. After ten minutes of assessing the situation, he stopped, folded his arms, and looked at Carrie. "Miss Wilson, I must tell you that I read about you in the Omaha newspaper. It was quite a story. You are one lucky soul. The good news is you're still alive. The bad news is it would be best if you live the rest of your life with the fragment remaining in your head. There is only one surgeon who might be able to remove the remains of that bullet. That is your doctor—Dr. Peterson."

Carrie knew the visit with Dr. Wheeler was a long-shot. She returned home disappointed with the news.

Chapter 6

December 15, 1914

*D*octor Andrew Peterson was nearing the time when he would graduate from the University of Minnesota Medical School. On December 15 the daily mail brought invitations to the Larson mailbox. Lewis and Jennie Larson received an invitation to Andrew's graduation exercises on January 16, 1915. Also included with the day's mail was an invitation addressed to Miss Carrie Wilson. Her letter did not have a return address on it, so she had no idea who sent it. Andrew figured she would not open it if she knew it was from him. With each invitation were round-trip train tickets. Andrew knew that not all of the family could attend because of farm chores.

Andrew also sent in Carrie's letter an invitation for her to attend a concert of the Minneapolis Symphony Orchestra that Saturday evening. He wasn't sure if she would attend but he sent it anyway. A note was attached to the ticket:

Carrie,

> *I would be honored if you would accompany me to this concert. You will be my date, as many of my medical friends are attending with dates or wives. You mentioned in your last communiqué that you are not interested in a personal*

relationship at this time. If you so desire, you may sit in a different location in the auditorium. If you wish, I will consider this night as my gift to you, a very good friend. You may consider the night simply as a chance to see a symphony orchestra perform. Make it whatever you wish. You have many options. Please consider attending with me or alone. I trust we are still friends, maybe even good friends.

Andrew.

Carrie thought about the letter and Andrew's desire to have her attend in whatever capacity. She suddenly had great compassion and sympathy for him. He was all alone in medical school. *Maybe it wouldn't hurt me to have some feeling for him for a couple of days,* she said to herself. *At least for Jennie and Lewis . . . they are so fond of him.*

Lewis and Jennie sent a letter to Andrew stating that they would attend the graduation along with Carrie. Andrew had written that arrangements had been made for them to stay two nights at a hotel along University Avenue near the Minneapolis campus where the indoor graduation exercises were to be held. Carrie would stay at the same location but would have a separate room. They would arrive on Friday afternoon, stay overnight at the hotel, attend Andrew's graduation on Saturday morning followed by a luncheon on Saturday noon, and return to Spring Prairie by Sunday afternoon.

Lewis and Jennie had not been to Minneapolis since they came through on their trip from Norway and Sweden to Spring Prairie Township with their families, both at different times during the 1880s. Many of their friends and relatives from the Old Country had settled in the Twin Cities—or close by—and this trip would give them the opportunity to see them once more.

Carrie still had mixed emotions about attending the concert as Andrew's date. She talked to Jennie about it one Saturday morning when the men were working with the cattle in the barnyard and the children were at the church practicing for their Christmas program.

"Carrie, I would consider it an honor to receive an invitation from a prominent up-and-coming physician who was also my doctor. On top of it, you will be attending a professional orchestra concert. That may never happen again in your lifetime. Whatever you and he have going on between you, you need to set it aside until after you attend the graduation and the concert."

"I guess it will be okay," Carrie replied. "It's just that I don't want to get too involved with Andrew. After what happened with my last relationship, I am frightened to get anywhere near a romance. I really think he is sweet on me. I have thought that ever since I found out he came to Spring Prairie to meet you while I was still in the hospital."

Jennie was a little puzzled. "Why would you not want to become involved?" she asked.

"Two reasons. First, my being a cripple will be a disability to Andrew. Second, Andrew and I do not see faith and religion in the same way."

"How do you know that?" Jennie asked.

"By his rigid and evasive reaction to comments I have made, and from what he's told me about his background," Carrie answered.

"Well, have you ever asked him directly about his faith?" Jennie asked.

"Not really," Carrie answered.

"Here is your chance to ask him . . . at his graduation or at the concert," Jennie suggested. "Actually, I cannot see how a medical doctor cannot have a faith. The human body is a miracle in itself. Andrew works with it every day. Just the miracle of birth is enough to make a nonbeliever believe if he thinks honestly about it."

"Jennie," Carrie responded, "you are so right."

"Besides, the entire weekend will be paid for," Jennie added with a wink and a smile.

That night Carrie wrote a letter to Andrew accepting his invitation to attend both the concert date and the graduation exercises. That same night Carrie prayed that God would give her wisdom and understanding into this particular subject with her doctor. She also prayed once more for Andrew in his quest to find the answer to how to remove the fragment of the bullet in her head.

Christmas 1914

The entire Larson family and Carrie all participated in the Zion Lutheran Church Christmas program. It was presented Christmas morning after the Swedish folk had their Julotta service. There were only eight full Swedish members in the church, along with fifteen who were part Swedish. This number included the Larson children. When the Norwegians saw the menu for the breakfast to be served after the Swedish Julotta service, they decided to attend the Christmas morning service along with the Swedes. Thus, it was made into a grand Scandinavian affair.

The breakfast meal was served at 7:00 a.m. and was something that the congregation had never experienced before. Both countries, Norway and Sweden, were represented with an abundance of various ethnic foods. There were Swedish meatballs, rollepolse (spicy pressed meat), mashed potatoes, three kinds of gravy, lnlagd sill (pickled herring), Yulekaka (Norwegian Christmas bread), risgrynsgrot (rice pudding), fruktsoppa (fruit soup), Svensk skorpor (Swedish rusks), and many kinds of ethnic breads and pastries. The food was eaten and washed down with plenty of egg coffee and spring water from across the road at the school. One ethnic item that was missing from the food table was lutefisk. The church board ruled against it soon after the church was formed because of its smell. The men wanted it, but the women voted against it.

One of the Norwegian men asked Jennie Larson what "Julotta" meant. "It means Christmas as the sun is rising," Jennie responded.

The weather made for a mild sunny Christmas Day. Each farm household had their own tradition of giving and receiving presents. There were some households that were without the funds to buy the food and presents to celebrate the day in the manner that was desired, due to hardships they had suffered throughout the year. Lewis and Jennie Larson seem to know who those families were. During the year they would put away some egg money for the purpose of helping these needy people, especially those with children. After a few years other families also started to help out those in need. It became a tradition for many of the folk at the Zion Lutheran Church to provide for the needy in the community.

In between Christmas and New Year's, Carrie was busy making the dress she would wear for Andrew's graduation and for their concert date. She had the fabric that she had gotten from her mother, and with Jennie's help the two of them designed it. "I think this dress will be beautiful, and you wearing it will make it even more beautiful," Lena said to Carrie.

"Thank you," Carrie responded. "I just hope I can keep it clean and pressed on the train, at the luncheon, and traveling through the snow. Maybe I can find a box to carry it in."

"I'll bet this is the nicest dress you have ever worn on a date, Carrie." Jennie stated.

Carrie looked at Jennie and then hung her head. "Jennie," Carrie replied, "I'm going to tell you a secret. You've probably suspected this, but this will be my first date with a man for several years."

Jennie had no comment and only gave Carrie a hug. She understood.

A few days before they were supposed to leave for Minneapolis, Lewis received a letter from Andrew with some last-minute information. "Thank you again for wanting to come to my graduation," he wrote, "it means so much to me."

The morning of January 15th arrived, and it was the time for Lewis, Jennie and Carrie to leave for the Twin Cities on the Northern Pacific passenger train. Freddie was going to take them to the train depot in time to catch the train arriving at 8:00 a.m. from the west.

As they arrived at the Stockwood depot, it started to snow and the wind began to blow. Freddie drove the team of horses pulling the covered sleigh. Suddenly the wind picked up more intensely, and Lewis advised Freddie to spend the day—and the night, if necessary—in the depot. Or at least wait until the wind died down before returning home.

The depot agent announced that a blizzard was approaching central Minnesota from the west, and that the train would be at the station fifteen minutes early in hopes that it would beat the storm. All of the passengers quickly boarded the train, and it departed the station promptly at 7:45 a.m.

As they began to speed up along the tracks, so did the wind accompanying the heavy snow. The passengers could barely see the telegraph poles along the tracks even though it was broad daylight. The train was starting to hit some of the drifts that were forming by the blowing snow. The impacts were getting more intense by the minute.

Lewis asked the conductor about these drifts "Aren't the engineers afraid that the train will derail if the engine hits the drifts too hard?"

"That's always a possibility," answered the elderly conductor. "But if we don't hit them hard, we may become stuck in a snow bank and may not be able to get out until the storm clears. I've been on some trains that have gotten stuck so bad that it took six of the big steam engines to pull us out."

The engines began to gain more speed to increase the momentum. The repetitive hitting of the snow banks began to lull many of the passengers into an intermittent sleep. Soon, most everyone was sleeping in their coach seats, as well as some in the dining and club cars.

They arrived at the Union Train Station in Minneapolis on Friday afternoon at 3:00 p.m. They were met by an enclosed motorized touring car, complete with driver, and Andrew. All of the suitcases were placed in the trunk, and the Larsons, Carrie, and Andrew climbed inside the warm vehicle.

Carrie and Andrew had not seen each other since their fall medical appointment. The only correspondence between them was the letter and invitations relating to the Minneapolis trip. When they first met, Andrew greeted Carrie warmly and kissed her hand. Lewis and Jennie had corresponded periodically with the doctor, so Andrew had been brought up to date with some of the events going on with their lives.

Although Carrie had been asked for dates several times by two of the more prominent bachelor young men in the township, she had refused to go. She had not even offered them a reason for her rejection. She just was not in the courting mood with the men in Spring Prairie Township, or anyone else, for that matter. Andrew, on the other hand, had dated a couple of young ladies he had met in his association with various university sororities. He was the most eligible bachelor within the medical student body. And despite the many available and eligible prospects, Carrie was still on his mind.

"Something has to happen to bring these two people closer together," Jennie whispered to Lewis. "Maybe this trip will cause it to happen. We'll think of something."

"Now, Jennie," Lewis replied, "let's let nature take its course. If it's supposed to happen, it will happen. You and I are a perfect example of that. Our meeting was not by chance, even though we could not understand each other's languages. Also, your parents could not accept me at first. But it was meant to be."

Saturday morning after the graduation, everyone was supposed to meet in a gathering room outside the big dining room at the hotel. Andrew was the first one to arrive. He wanted to meet and greet each person as they made their appearance. Andrew had invited a total of fifteen guests, including his parents and a brother. They had arrived Thursday afternoon on a train from Iowa. Two of Andrew's physician partners and their wives, the head of the clinic where they worked, two of Andrew's women acquaintances, and three student friends of his completed the guest list. The women acquaintances were nurses Andrew had worked with and had dated on occasion.

The Larsons and Carrie were the first of the guests to arrive. They waited in the gathering room for the other guests to make their appearance. Jennie suddenly had an idea. She was familiar with formal gatherings such as the one she was about to participate in. When she worked at the Buffalo River Mansion, it was customary for them to place name placards for each guest at the table in the dining room for formal events. She walked into the dining hall and looked for a large round table. There it was, at a corner of the room. Jennie counted the place settings. There were sixteen—one for Andrew and each of his fifteen special guests. She walked around the table to find Andrew's name. It was on the far side. On either side of his place setting were the names of two doctors. Three places from one of them was the name "Carrie Wilson."

Jennie looked around to make sure none of the hotel staff were watching and quickly changed some of the names around. Carrie was now going to be sitting by her doctor Andrew Peterson. Jennie was on the other side of Andrew. She had done this many times before when she was working at the mansion at the secret request of a guest. She walked back into the gathering room with a big smile. No one would know the difference, nor would anyone care.

Soon the other guests began to arrive. Everyone was dressed very formally. Carrie was wearing her newly sewn pink silk dress that she and Jennie had designed and made. A pearl necklace that Andrew had given her for a Christmas present adorned her neck. She had been tempted to send it back to him when she opened it, but Jennie talked her into keeping it. She wore it as a courtesy to Andrew, but she hoped no one would ask her where she got it. She figured Andrew may get into a little trouble if his medical school advisors found out he was associating with one of his patients.

Andrew then led everyone into the big dining room. He read off each guest's name as he circled the big round table. Each of the guests in turn took their seat. Andrew saw that Carrie needed help with her wheelchair and was there to assist her. "Let me help you," he offered. Once he was seated next to her he asked, "Is your room okay? Did you sleep well last night? Are you enjoying your trip so far?"

"I am fine and I'm having a good time," she answered. "The room is beautiful, thank you."

All were seated and Andrew stood and addressed his guests. "I wish to thank you all for coming this noon. I am going to ask my friend Jennie Larson to ask the blessing on the meal that will be set before us."

Jennie looked at Andrew and smiled. She had prayed that he would do this. They all lowered their heads. Jennie stood and prayed the first prayer that she had learned in Smaaland, Sweden, as a little girl. "I Jesu namn till bords vi gå, välsigna Gud den mat vi få. Gud till ära, oss till gagn, så få vi mat i Jesu namn."

"Thank you, Jennie," Andrew said. "Will you now translate what you just prayed for all of us who do not speak Swedish?"

Jennie remained standing and spoke in clear, Swedish-accented English, "In Jesus' name to the table we go, God bless the food we receive. To God the honor, us the gain, so we have food in Jesus' name."

Carrie touched Andrew's sleeve. "Thank you for doing that. It added a spiritual touch to this occasion."

"Well, Carrie, you are a positive influence on me," Andrew replied.

"How is that?" she asked.

"Well, let me tell you. Our talks in the Moorhead hospital have had an effect on my medical practice. When I was in Switzerland last summer, I performed many operations. About six months ago, I was facing a particularly difficult operation on a head injury. I didn't know what to do as I was faced with an unforeseen situation. My thoughts suddenly turn to you. I said to myself, *Maybe I should follow Carrie's example and pray.* So I did. Not only did I pray for myself, I also prayed for the patient. I felt almost as if you were there praying with me."

"Maybe it was the angels that were with you," Carrie replied. "I often pray that they come down to guide me."

"Carrie, I believe you're right. But I also believe that your brave spirit was with me. I want to apologize for the unbelieving comments about angels I made to you in the past."

Carrie suddenly had a feeling of warmth and peace come over her at what Andrew had shared with her.

Soon the several courses of food were being served for the meal. Everyone was engaged in talking to the person or persons next to them. Carrie glanced at the two women sitting directly across the table from her. They were watching Carrie and Andrew. She could almost see what they were thinking by the looks on their faces. *What is that crippled woman doing by my boyfriend?* Carrie just smiled back. She suspected they probably had known Andrew on more than just a professional basis.

The meal took an hour. It consisted of a salad, fruit juice, meat, potatoes, vegetables, rolls, and a layer cake with ice cream. Jennie thought they should have served pickled herring and Lewis thought lutefisk would have been fitting. The plates, glasses, coffee cups, and dinnerware were of excellent pattern; and the tablecloth and napkins were of the highest quality linen.

Afterward, there were a few introductions and greetings from some of the guests. All had congratulations and well-wishes for Andrew. Andrew stood up and spoke briefly about Carrie. She never expected it.

"Many of you probably heard or read the news almost two years ago about a teacher in a western Minnesota country school who was shot several times by an estranged boyfriend. The good news is that she survived the attack despite being shot several times. I happened to be at the hospital where she was brought in and was chosen to operate on her. That woman is here as one of my guests this afternoon."

As the crowd began to applaud, Carrie tried to stand up. Andrew reached down and helped Carrie stand up. Andrew held her around her waist as the rest of the guests stood and applauded. Then he helped her sit down and continued, "Carrie has lived with a pioneer family since she began teaching at the Spring Prairie Township School, and I have become very good friends with them. When I first met them, I was able to repay their kind hospitality toward me by saving their best workhorse after he had gorged himself on a patch of wild mushrooms. The entire family got involved and together we saved Molly. They welcomed me into their home and treated me as if I were one of the family. I am grateful and humbled that they would share this very important day with me, and I am privileged to call them my friends."

Thank you all for coming today and I hope you enjoy the rest of your time here."

After the luncheon, Carrie and Andrew sat together in the hotel lobby and talked for two hours. Lewis and Jennie spent the same two hours visiting with friends and relatives who had also immigrated from Norway and Sweden and were living in the Twin Cities area. They were divided into two groups, of course — those who spoke Norwegian and those who spoke Swedish.

Andrew wanted to ask Carrie a question. He didn't especially want to mix business with pleasure, but since he hadn't seen Carrie for a while he needed to risk it. After all, she was his favorite patient. "So, Carrie," Andrew started the conversation, "how have you been feeling lately?"

"Everything is fine," she answered her doctor instinctively. She was afraid he would ask about the Omaha doctor whom she had seen in August about the bullet fragment in her head.

"How are you managing with the wheelchair? Is it hard to move around the schoolroom or move from the wheelchair to the crutches? Do you have trouble keeping discipline among the active boys and girls?"

"The children seem to have more respect for me as compared to before the shooting. The older children help out, which is typical in all country schools. There are times when the younger children have trouble behaving themselves. The boys want to show off for the girls, and the girls have their favorite boys. It all makes teaching very interesting . . . and sometimes a little challenging."

"Do you get out much?" Andrew asked, not thinking how Carrie may take that question.

Carrie looked at Andrew as if she were somewhat taken aback by his question. Andrew could see that he had asked the wrong thing. "Let me rephrase that question. What I mean is, can you get around the farm like you did before?"

"I thought that you meant something else," she said, trying to stifle her laughter, but Andrew saw an opportunity to inquire into that particular subject also.

"Well," Andrew said, "Let's talk about that also. You're a very attractive woman, and I imagine the men in Spring Prairie are thinking about you and watching you at every social function you attend. Have you been associating socially with male companions?"

Carrie was not expecting that bold question from her doctor. She thought about ignoring the question and changing the subject, but she changed her mind. "I have had a few male individuals who have asked me out—nothing very serious. Not too many men want a woman who isn't able to walk. But I expect that to change one of these days . . . when I walk again."

Andrew and Carrie looked at each other and wondered where this particular subject would go in their conversation. Then Carrie added, "Of course, there are some of my older male students who, I think, are captivated by my presence and keep their eyes on me. I believe I have developed eyes in the back of my head."

"That could be," Andrew laughed. "They say that when one function of your body goes kaput, another increases in its function. I have been witness to that phenomenon, especially with blind people."

Ever since Andrew had first seen this beautiful country schoolteacher on the gurney at the hospital, he had been intrigued by her. The feeling was not mutual, however. Carrie thought of Andrew as a handsome man—a good doctor with a great career ahead of him—someone who would make a great husband and father. But she had no desire to get involved with him romantically. It would take another miracle for her to do so. Carrie had been through a dreadful experience with a man who had nearly killed her and had left her unable to walk. But there were other issues, too, and Carrie decided it was the right time for her to bring up the most important issue that she had with Andrew on a personal level. She looked directly into her doctor's eyes and said, "Andrew, let me ask you a personal question."

"Ask away," he said, "whatever you wish to know."

"What is your religious background, Andrew?"

Andrew diverted his eyes to the other side of the hotel lobby. He knew this question would eventually come up in his relationship with Carrie, and he had often contemplated what his answer would be. He returned his attention to her and said in a direct manner, "Let me answer your question with a question for you. Does religion make that much of a difference in a relationship?"

Carrie thought that was what his answer would be. She expected it. She was ready with an answer. "Yes, it most certainly does make a difference."

"What difference does it make?" he asked her, although he knew he was risking making Carrie view him negatively with his response.

"That answer tells me what your religious background is," she commented. It was a direct answer to Andrew, and she knew that he would probably be hurt by her answer. He was. He once again looked away and was quiet for a full minute. The only sounds audible were the people walking up the long stairway adjacent to where they were seated and the various conversations taking place around them.

Carrie finally broke the silence. "Andrew, can I ask you another question with the risk of further offending you?" She knew she was on thin ice to someone who was her physician, a good friend, and was kind enough to invite her for a weekend she never could have experienced without his generosity. They were also about to go to a formal concert together—their first official date. They both knew that if they were ever to have a second date, their conversation would need to turn positive quickly. He continued to look away.

Without his consent, she asked the question anyway, "Let's say that you met a woman whom you desired to marry. You loved each other, got married, and decided to have children. Where would you take the children to church and Sunday school? If you couldn't agree on a church, would you and your wife each take them to different churches? Would you flip a coin? And what else would you not agree on?"

Andrew suddenly realized where the discussion was going and that Carrie was correct in her logic. He needed to terminate it before either of them caused more hurt feelings. "I don't want to say anymore for fear of offending you further. Just let me say that I admire your faith and wish I had what you have. I think you will be the perfect wife for some young man someday. Personally, I wish that man would be me. But I know that it may never come to pass. I doubt very much that I could come up to the standard that you need and desire." Andrew took Carrie's right hand and kissed it. "We need to get going so we're not late for the concert."

Andrew pushed Carrie in her wheelchair five blocks to Symphony Hall on the university campus. Carrie was very quiet and knew that she and Andrew were not feeling comfortable with how their discussion had ended. *How can I make amends for the hurt feelings I may have caused?* they both asked to themselves.

Carrie had never been to an event such as a symphony orchestra concert. What she was wearing fit in very well with the dresses worn by the other ladies in attendance. She had managed to keep the dress clean, which was her primary concern. Their tickets were for seats on the main floor, so there were no stairs to climb. Andrew pushed Carrie's wheelchair to their assigned seats, which were on the aisle of the tenth row from the front.

"Andrew, you put some thought into getting these seats! That was very considerate of you."

"I just wanted to make this experience one that you would always remember," he replied as he helped her from her wheelchair into her seat. Andrew returned the wheelchair to the lobby and then joined Carrie in the concert hall. He was still feeling the hurt from what Carrie had said to him at the hotel. They were both quiet as they sat in their seats and listened to the orchestra warming up.

Andrew broke the silence between them by briefly telling Carrie about the program that night. It was to be an all-Dvorak concert. "Carrie, did you know Dvorak's family lived a couple of summers in the town of Spillville, Iowa? It's just a few miles from where I was born and raised."

"Really?" Carrie replied. "Have you been to the town?"

"Not yet, but I intend to stop there next summer when I go home to visit my family," Andrew answered.

They spent the next five minutes reading the program before Andrew broke the silence once again. "Carrie, I need to tell you about a breakthrough procedure that our team of doctors has developed in the removal of objects from the head."

Carrie quickly directed her attention from the program to Andrew and became interested in that particular subject. "Oh, please tell me about it!"

"We have yet to perform it on a patient, but that will be the next step."

Just then the concertmaster walked on the stage and the concert began. Various times during the concert Andrew reached over and gently took Carrie's hand. This helped to soften the tension between them that was created during the discussion they had started and left unfinished at the hotel.

During the intermission, Andrew decided to revisit their earlier conversation from a different angle. "Tell me, Carrie . . . I have never been to the Zion Lutheran Church. Are Jennie and Lewis quite involved with it?"

"Yes, Lewis is the church klokker," she answered.

"What in the world is a church klokker?" Andrew asked.

"The klokker is a layman who basically assists the pastor and leads the congregation in singing of the hymns," Carrie answered. "Some klokkers are also responsible for ringing the church bell. I believe the word and the job comes from the Old Country. I had never heard of it until I came to Spring Prairie. That's one thing I enjoy about going to church and studying the Bible. I'm always learning something new."

The concert ended with Carrie fighting back sleep. She was still tired from the rough train ride from the previous day. They stayed in their seats until most of the crowd had filed out. A few of Andrew's colleagues, along with their dates, visited with them for a few minutes. One stately looking young woman was especially noticeable to Carrie. She gave Carrie a glaring stare.

As Andrew was pushing the wheelchair out of the building, Carrie asked Andrew about the woman with the stare. "She is a woman with whom I had a blind date about seven months ago. It was our first and last date. She wanted to date more, but I just wasn't interested. I think she's still a little angry about it."

"Well," Carrie replied, "I just gave her a big smile."

"Good move, Carrie," Andrew replied with a laugh. "Good move."

Andrew wheeled Carrie back to the hotel and to her room. "I hope you enjoyed the evening," he said to her.

She turned and looked at him, not able to hide the tears streaming down her face. "I'm very sorry for what I said to you that may have made you disappointed and unhappy."

"Don't be," he said, "I'm glad you said it. Coming from you I know it's the truth. I need someone like you in my life to tell me the honest truth. No one else has ever been as straightforward with me as you have. And it's best that it be said now so that we don't have any misunderstandings in any relationship. You are someone very special and soon you will find someone as special as you are. I know it." Andrew helped Carrie by unlocking her hotel door and again kissed her hand. He then left the hotel and returned to his dorm room.

Carrie had trouble getting to sleep. She felt bad and decided to get up and write Andrew a letter.

Andrew,

Thank you for the evening. It was wonderful. I am just sorry for how it ended between us. I made you feel bad on many levels. But like you said, I believe what was said needed to be said before any further relationship ties between us commence. At this point you need to be my doctor and I need to be your patient, and that is all.

Warmest heartfelt congratulations on your graduation from medical school, and best wishes for the great
career that is before you. I will pray for you every day.

Carrie.

In the morning Carrie asked Lewis to deliver the letter to
Andrew at the dorm where he was staying down the street.

As the train made its way through central Minnesota to the
Stockwood station, Jennie sensed that something was bothering
Carrie. "Is everything okay, Carrie?" she asked. "You seem so
quiet."

Carrie didn't wish to get Jennie or Lewis involved in her
problems with Andrew. "I guess I am a little tired from all of the
excitement of the past few days."

"You and Andrew must have had a long talk last night,"
Jennie said. "We think the world of him. I know the children
love him."

Carrie said nothing and just looked out the window of the
Northern Pacific Railroad passenger car. Her silence told Jennie
most of the story.

Carrie had 250 miles of railroad travel time to think about
her life, her situation, the past three days, and about Andrew
Peterson.

Chapter 7

February 10, 1915

*I*n four days it would be Valentine's Day, and it was going to be a big day at the Spring Prairie Township School. The students had been busy in their homes and in class making Valentines for their fellow students, their teacher, their parents, and some of their neighbors. The Larson children, with the encouragement of mother Jennie, had made extra Valentines. These were for the students whose parents would not help their children make Valentines. Jennie was aware of these children, their parents, and the situations they were in. Teacher Miss Carrie was also familiar with the difficulties of many of the township's families.

Jennie would always bring a meal and visit with any of the township's new immigrant farm residents. She would find out if any help was needed with the children or in the home. If there were a major project that was needed to aid in the new family's success in their new residence, she would volunteer to organize it. Many times she would alert the ladies group at the Zion Lutheran Church, and they would make it into a work project — projects like: getting shoes for children, purchasing school supplies, obtaining winter clothes, providing basic food and filling various other needs. Sometimes when sicknesses occurred in the home, a helping hand was provided to get the family through it.

Carrie awoke on the morning of February 10 and was experiencing some discomfort in her back and legs. This was not the first time. The distress in her neck and back had begun about the first of February. At first she wasn't too concerned and tried to brush it off. But it had started to get worse. She decided to tell Jennie. They were eating breakfast, and Lewis was out completing the chores with the boys. "Jennie, my back and legs are starting to hurt at night."

Jennie stopped eating her piece of toast with jam and stared at Carrie. "How long has this been going on?" she asked.

Carrie knew where the discussion would lead and what the next step would be. Andrew had predicted this and had told Jennie and Lewis, as well as Carrie, to watch for these symptoms.

"For about two weeks now . . . since the first of February," Carrie answered. "The pain is worse at night if I suddenly move my head on the pillow."

At that point Lewis walked into the kitchen from the shanty where he had removed his coat and boots. He walked over to the sink and washed his hands. Jennie went to the stove and filled a plate with scrambled eggs, bacon, and toast, then placed the assembled meal at Lewis's place at the table. Lewis sat down at the table. He closed his eyes and prayed silently asking the Lord's blessing on the food.

Jennie turned to Carrie. "Carrie, tell Lewis what you just told me."

Carrie was a little hesitant to tell Lewis about her discomfort, since he more than Jennie was following her post-surgery condition. He had been in communication with Andrew via mail. Andrew had told him that the bullet in Carrie's head most likely would move in time and may cause some pain or further physical impairment. But the doctor also told him that Carrie would, when this happened, begin to experience feeling in her legs once again.

"I have begun to have pain in my back and in my legs and feet at night."

Lewis thought for a moment and then said, "Carrie, you know what this may mean."

"It means that the bullet in my head is doing something . . . either moving or causing some infection."

Jennie was the next to speak with the expected phrase. "We need to make an appointment with the doctors."

"What doctors?" Carrie uttered in a subdued tone.

Lewis's next words were on the tip of his tongue. "The best doctor available," he quickly answered.

Carrie and Jennie both knew who Lewis meant. Dr. Andrew Peterson.

Carrie was aware that Andrew was the best in his field within at least five hundred miles of Spring Prairie and he was working on patients suffering from similar types of injuries. She was well aware that many of his patients, because of the severity of their injuries, never survived once they came to him. Many times they died before they even got to the hospital. She also knew that she had no other option. "I just wonder if he is ready to perform this type of operation," Carrie said.

"What did he tell you when you talked to him at his graduation?" Jennie asked.

"We really did not discuss that particular subject," Carrie answered. "We were engaged in discussion on other subjects."

"I can just imagine what that was all about," Jennie smilingly replied.

Lewis continued the discussion. "I think you need to see some doctor—any doctor—in Moorhead."

"I guess you're right," Carrie admitted. "Lewis, will you contact the doctor's office today by phone? I guess this is what I have been expecting. See if you can make an appointment for Saturday so I won't have to miss school. The children don't like having a substitute teacher, especially the one they had when we went to Minneapolis."

"What is it you were expecting?" Jennie asked.

"The movement of the bullet that will necessitate an operation," Carrie responded with some hesitancy. "It's supposed to happen and it's going to happen."

Lewis caught Carrie's comment. He usually was not as attentive to the family conversation around the dinner table as his wife wanted him to be. But this one he was aware of. "What do you mean 'it's supposed to happen'?" Lewis asked.

Carrie suddenly realized she had mistakenly let the cat out of the bag and hinted at her secret. She was slow in responding to her landlord with an answer.

"Well," Lewis inquired impatiently, "will you tell us what is supposed to happen?"

"Yes, I will," Carrie finally answered. "It's about a dream I had back in the hospital when Andrew operated on me and took the bullets out. I had an out-of-body experience. I think that's the term they use for it. I really don't want to . . ."

Just then the outside door opened and in walked one of the many neighbors bringing a large casserole. It was a repayment to Jennie for helping them the month before. Jennie had taken care of their children overnight when they needed to go to Fargo.

This subject needs to be further discussed, Lewis concluded to himself. Then he said to Carrie, "We will make an appointment with the hospital in Moorhead today for as soon as they can get you in. They will contact Dr. Andrew. I must warn you that he may stop in here for a visit. I'm sure you wouldn't mind that. He likes to visit us for some strange reason."

Carrie did not respond.

That night before bed, Carrie sat down and wrote Andrew a letter. It had been several weeks since either of them had written. Carrie had the idea that he had some female friends where he was working and that he may be occupied with them. *That's fine with me,* she said to herself. It had been almost a month since she had seen him at his graduation, and the two of them did not separate on the best of terms.

She didn't know how to start the letter. *I guess I should just start and pour out my concern and feelings,* she thought to herself.

Andrew,

 I trust that all is well and you're doing well in your practice and research. The reason for my letter: By now you may have heard from the Moorhead hospital. I have begun to feel discomfort in my back and head. I think the bullet may be moving. I can almost feel it moving, although it may be just my imagination. I will see someone at the doctor's office as soon as we can get in. Maybe it's nothing serious, but we need to make sure.

 Thank you again for your hospitality on your graduation weekend. I will always have fond memories of the special time we shared together, and I enjoyed getting to know you and your family better. I especially enjoyed hearing about your work and research in head injuries and surgery, although the pictures in my mind were a little frightening. I also enjoyed telling you about my work with the children. It was so nice to be able to talk to someone who is interested in listening to me, other than my Spring Prairie family.

 I look forward to our next meeting and continued conversation.

Carrie

* * * * *

 The next morning at the breakfast table Jennie said to Carrie, "I don't have an out-of-body dream to tell you about, but I do have a story about seeing a ghost one night. The experience was so real that I wasn't even scared. We've got a few minutes before you have to leave for school, and I want to tell you the story."

 "I can use a good ghost story," Carrie responded with a chuckle. "Go on . . . tell me."

Jennie took a sip of her special tea and started the story. "I was at the Buffalo River Mansion where I worked, and I couldn't sleep one night. There was a blizzard roaring outside. The wind and snow were whistling around and through the tiny mansion cracks and crevices producing a chorus of ghostly sounds that would even scare the wits out of a rattlesnake. I was walking down the winding stairway from the second floor. All of a sudden and out of nowhere, a figure appeared in the middle of the large dining hall. I had cleaned up earlier from a special dinner for the group of guests from Chicago. They were planning on continuing their travels to the West Coast in the morning on the Northern Pacific passenger train. The blizzard would ensure that their stay at the Mansion would be extended by at least another day.

"I had never seen the owner of the mansion . . . only his wife. He died shortly before I began work at the mansion. Abigail Wass was the one who hired both Lewis and me. Her husband was Captain Warren Wass. Prior to his death he spent much of his time traveling. He was a hero for the Union Army during the Civil War. His family had a manufacturing plant in Vermont which was converted to producing armaments for the Union Army during the war. The family was well-rewarded after the war, and the Captain inherited all of his family's wealth. That was how he was able to buy the land and build the mansion. After the war he spent some time traveling the lecture circuit speaking on the Civil War and its causes.

"Back to my ghost story: I didn't know it at the time, but the ghost was the captain wearing his uniform, complete with all of his medals shiny buttons, and gold insignias. He walked across the room very slowly toward the big oak table. I thought that big old table would stop his forward motion, but I was wrong. He walked right through the table and chairs. Or maybe the table and chairs went through him. When he got to the middle of the table, he stopped. He looked right at me and said, "Jennie, you are doing a good job. Tell Abigail to give you a raise."

Carrie was starting to disbelieve the story she was hearing from Jennie. "Did you get a raise?" she asked Jennie.

"Well," continued Jennie, "the next morning I went to Abigail and told her what I had seen and heard. She was very interested and asked many detailed questions about how the ghost was dressed, how he looked, and his pronunciation of words. I answered her as best I could remember. She waited a short time after I was done talking and really surprised me. 'That was my husband, Warren,' she told me. 'I talk to him quite often myself.'"

After a momentary pause Jennie said to Carrie, "Now, I don't know if you believe my story any more than I will believe your story, but I can tell you Abigail did give me that raise. So are you going to tell me about your out-of-body dream?"

"Yes," Carrie responded, "and I will add your vision to my book of dreams."

* * * * *

Freddie drove the sleigh to school that Valentine's Day. The weather was mild after a light snow. As the sleigh was moving, Carrie thought about her condition and longed for the time when she could walk again. Maybe soon.

The sun was just rising when they got to the driveway of the school. Freddie carried Carrie into the school and set into the wheelchair that was kept at the school. She had a wheelchair at the Larson farm home, one at the school, and one at the church.

As she sat behind her desk, she thought about what she would encounter that day with the children. Every day was a new and exciting experience in the country school. *Something new is bound to happen today,* Carrie thought to herself.

This morning's Scripture reading was the Thirteenth Chapter of I Corinthians — the love chapter. As always, the children were given a chance to ask questions about what was just read. That particular morning two questions were asked. Harold Hansen asked, "Why is love so important?"

Carrie thought for a moment as she looked out the window to the county road on the north side of the school. She needed an answer that everyone could understand. The children sometimes came up with the most difficult questions! After a few moments of contemplation, Carrie was ready with an answer. "Love is a God-given emotion and feeling that causes people to live peaceably with God and each other. God loves us and He wants us to love Him. Then we will love others and live peaceably among them."

Carrie stopped there and put her Bible on the desk. She saw some puzzlement on the faces of some of her students. That's when the second question was asked.

"Why then is there so much hatred in the world?" asked Louise Larson. "People hate each other and they sometimes want to kill each other." Louise stopped abruptly. She realized what she had just said in front of her teacher. "Oh . . . I'm sorry, Miss Wilson."

"Louise, don't apologize. That's okay. You have brought up a subject that I would like to discuss with the class. A man tried to shoot me almost two years ago in this school. Many of you were in this room when it happened. There was so much hatred in that man's heart, and he felt he needed to express that hatred . . . to get back at someone. In this case it was me that he wanted to get back at." Carrie wanted to stop the discussion at that point, but that was not going to happen.

"Why did that man hate you?" George Lindquist asked.

Now Carrie was trapped. How was she going to answer this question to her students, half of whom were under twelve years of age? She sent up a quick prayer request to heaven. Then she fanned the class with her eyes.

"I knew that man for a short time. I liked him at first. He was very nice to me, and he treated me with courtesy and respect. But then he started to be mean to me. I tried to remove myself from his company, but he kept following me. When I told him I did not want him to have contact with me, he believed it was because I was in love with another man. That wasn't true, but it was the story he made up and believed. He began to have bad feelings toward me. Not only did he begin to hate me but he began to hate himself. He believed he couldn't live without me. The only way he could think of to resolve this problem was to take both of our lives. So you see, class, this is where hatred can lead."

With that Carrie stopped the discussion. She wheeled her chair over to the front of the class to begin the art lesson for that day.

The rest of the morning passed without incident. At one o'clock in the afternoon it was time for the annual Valentine party. A heart-shaped box was filled with everyone's Valentines. The children's imagination went into creating most of the Valentines. Some of the envelopes were bulging, indicating that there was a piece of candy or a sucker inside. Carrie had handed out a list with each student's name so everyone in the class would have the correct spelling. The Valentines were in English, Swedish, and Norwegian. Normally, Carrie only permitted the class to use English when in school, but they would be able to use the same design and printing to make Valentine's for their Swedish and Norwegian family members and neighbors.

There were two children from a Hungarian family that had just moved to Spring Prairie from Montana. They were not familiar with our Valentine custom. Carrie was aware of this and assumed that they would not have any Valentines to give, but also that they may not get any. Carrie had kept the two children inside during the morning recess and had them sign their names to a Valentine for each of the other students. She also explained the American custom and the story of Saint Valentine. Their mother came that morning and helped with the translation. She spoke enough English to explain to the two children what the special day was all about. The two newcomers were overjoyed when they received their Valentines. After the Valentines were passed out, a boxful of decorated cupcakes was passed out for the students.

Many of Carrie's students had expressed an interest in learning more about the sinking of the Titanic. It had been almost three years since the terrible tragedy. After the Valentine's party she decided to read excerpts from a New York newspaper of the account of the ship on its first and final voyage. The students were fascinated as she read what happened when the massive ship hit the iceberg in the north Atlantic.

Many questions followed the reading. Margaret Peterson had the most interesting and perceptive question: "Did the people onboard have any practice of getting into the lifeboats?"

Carrie thought a moment. "Well, Margaret, I would say probably not. The article doesn't tell us. It does tell us that they never had enough lifeboats for everyone. Maybe a hundred years from now the historians will have better answers to some of our questions."

Many of the students expressed their interest in reading the entire article some other day during their free time.

When Carrie arrived home that evening, there was an over-sized letter waiting for her that had come in the mail. It was postmarked St. Paul, Minnesota. She assumed the letter was from Andrew. She opened the larger-than-normal envelope and pulled out a Valentine. Carrie stopped with a jolt. The thought never crossed her mind that Andrew would ever send her a Valentine. Plus, she had been so busy with the children's Valentine's Day activities that the thought of Andrew had completely slipped her mind. Of more importance to Carrie was the fact that this was a case of a doctor getting involved with his patient, and it should not be done.

His Valentine to her was a very thoughtfully handmade artistic endeavor. Carrie felt honored and humbled that he had taken so much time out of his busy schedule to cut and glue various pieces of colored construction paper and small white hand-made snowflakes into an elaborate card design. He could have just as easily bought a nice Valentine at a department store in Minneapolis. The verse he composed was especially thoughtful.

To Carrie,

The snowflakes in the air land on my coat for me to see.
They remind me of how pure your heart is to me.
If I could secure your heart, think of what our future could be.

All I need from you to secure your heart, is the key.
Happy Valentine's Day!

From Andrew

I wonder if Andrew sent his girlfriends a similar Valentine,
Carrie thought. *I would doubt it. This card had to have taken*
him hours to make. What should I do with it—send it back? That
would be a huge insult to him. Maybe I should make him one. But
that would give him a wrong impression of my feelings for him.
Maybe I should just send him a simple Thank You note.

The more Carrie thought about her neglect in sending something to him, the worse she felt. She carried the Valentine into
the kitchen and showed it to mother Jennie. Jennie fingered the
artwork and read the verse two times. "I think your doctor is
really sweet on you, Carrie. But I have known that for a long
time. I'll bet you sent him a beautiful card."

"Jennie, I completely forgot about it," Carrie replied. "I
can't figure out if I should feel terrible about it or not. After all,
he could get into real trouble for fraternizing with a patient. I
don't want to encourage that. But on the other hand, I never
even thought about sending him anything, and I'm feeling very
guilty about that."

"You need to sit down and write a letter to him," Jennie commented. "It's incredible to me that a busy doctor would take
the time to hand-make a card like that. You are someone very
special to him. Hold on to him, Carrie."

That night Carrie did write a letter to Andrew and then
stayed up until two in the morning making a special Valentine
entitled—To a friend. She hoped that it would be special enough
for him, and that it would compensate for her not getting a Valentine to him on time. She planned on mailing it in the mailbox
the next morning. It was four in the morning before she was
asleep.

* * * * *

The morning after Valentine's Day started out beautiful and sunny. The children at the country school were expecting to spend both the morning and afternoon recess periods playing in the snow. The snow that had fallen the night before was moist and ideal for making a snowman and building a snow fort.

The girls built a snowman on the south side of the school, and the boys built the snow fort on the north side. Miss Carrie allowed an extra ten minutes for each of the two recess periods for these group activities. All of the students were involved. If anyone had asked her why she took an extra twenty minutes out of school learning time for these activities, she would have answered, "This is where my students learn to work together as a community on a project, this time the community being the group of students themselves. They learn to work together."

What Carrie and the students did not know was what was in store for them after the afternoon recess. It would add to their learning in ways that they could never imagine.

Shortly after the students came in from the afternoon recess, it started snowing. The snow was light at first, but within fifteen minutes the snowfall had increased in intensity. Then the wind started blowing. Carrie opened the front door of the school and could not see the flagpole fifty feet away. Soon the heavy snow was accumulating on the ground at an alarming rate. Harold Hansen asked, "Miss Wilson, how are we going to get home tonight? This snow will soon be too deep for the horses to get through. The drivers will not be able to see the roads."

"Yes, indeed," Carrie said to her wise student, "we may have to stay here tonight."

It was soon 3:30, the time when some of the parents normally were outside the school to pick up the children. The fact that no parents had yet shown up was a strong indication that none would show up. Carrie decided to talk to the children concerning the weather situation. She gathered them around the potbelly stove and tried her best to put their minds at ease. "Children, it appears that we may have to stay in the schoolhouse tonight. And I cannot let any of you leave the building without a security rope tied around your waist or your chest, even to go to the outhouse. This is to keep you from wandering off and getting lost. Because none of your parents have come yet, we have to assume the weather is too bad to permit any travel.

"I will send two of you older boys over to the church horse barn sometime before dark to feed the horses and give them water. We can sleep on both sides of the room—girls on the north side, boys on the south side. I believe we have enough quilts and blankets in the quilt closet so that you can all lie on a quilt and have one covering you. I'll keep the stove going all night. I will also lock the door from the inside to prevent anyone from going out, in case any of you walk in your sleep. Do you have any questions?"

The room was quiet for a full thirty seconds. The winter winds were howling through the schoolhouse peaks causing an eerie sound. Fear showed on the faces of some of the children.

"What about our supper?" Queenie Halvorson asked.

"That is a good question, Queenie," Miss Wilson responded. "Does anyone have any suggestions?"

Max Perkins raised his hand. "Yes, Max?" Carrie said.

"My mother sent me with an entire loaf of fresh bread this morning. Maybe we could cut it into slices, and I will share it with everybody."

"Thank you for that offer, Max." Carrie answered. "Maybe others of us have some of our noon lunch left over that we could share."

Richard Gustafson spoke up. "I have two cans of Vienna sausages that are unopened. I'll place them on the spelling bench. Max, you can place your bread there also."

Soon the bench was covered with food collected from the students' lunch pails. The atmosphere of fear of the blizzard was replaced by the spirit of cooperation and survival. They began to play games, color pictures, write stories and sing songs.

Just when the students were starting to clean up from their supper there was a knock at the outside door. Everyone froze and looked at the teacher.

"Who could be knocking at this time of the evening in this kind of weather?" Carrie asked out loud. She got out of her chair and, using her crutches, moved cautiously toward the door. Just before she reached the door she said, "George, will you come and help me open the door?" George was the largest boy in the school. Carrie had a flashback of two years earlier, and she imagined many of her students did, too.

Within a minute both student and teacher were positioned on either side of the outside door. Carrie removed the key from her pocket and cautiously unlocked the door. George pushed the snow-blocked door open. A snow-covered man emerged from the outside and stumbled into the room half-frozen. As he took a few steps, the snow began to drop off in large amounts from his thin coat and pants onto the floor of the entryway. He had only a thin cap protecting his head, and he had a towel wrapped around his ears to protect them from the cold. He was a small man carrying a cloth bag and shivering with cold. The children just stared at him with expressions of surprise and pity. The man tried to say something to Carrie. He was out of breath and could not speak for several moments. Finally he warmed up enough to say, "Miss, please may I rest here for a little while? I am cold, thirsty, hungry, and tired. Can you help me?"

Carrie recognized that a teaching opportunity had just been thrust upon her country school class in the year 1915. Of any education that her children could learn in her classroom, none would be more important and beneficial in their lives than that of helping this poor soul. *This moment is no chance situation occurring at this time,* she thought to herself. It was only two days ago that she read to the class from the book of Hebrews that sometimes the Lord sends down angels in the form of people in distress to test us—to see if we have compassion and true love for people.

Carrie needed to set the class at ease and provide the man with a sense of welcome. Holding her crutches in one hand, she put her free arm around the man's shoulders and gave him a warm hug. He smiled broadly and tears began to flow down both of his cheeks, melting the fresh snow still on them. She released him and quickly grabbed her crutches so that she wouldn't fall to the floor. "Please come and sit down by the fire," the teacher said. "Louise, will you get our guest a glass of water?"

"Yes, I will, Miss Wilson," Louise answered as she walked to the water tank. Carrie needed to quickly get all of the class involved with this caring mission. It was a giant opportunity.

"Someone, please fill up a plate of food for our guest. What is your name, sir?" Carrie asked the strange man.

"My name is Victor Meland, and I am from Detroit, Michigan. I was riding on the train on my way to Canada when someone gave me some wrong directions. I started walking and it started snowing real hard. If I hadn't found this schoolhouse, I may have frozen to death." The man stopped there and took a swig of water. "Thank you, Louise," he said.

Maxine Olson took a clean empty plate that was sitting on Miss Carrie's desk and placed some of the food on it from the spelling bench and gave it to the man. Soon Mr. Meland was eating like he hadn't eaten in days. Miss Carrie knew that he was also very tired.

"Ok, children," she said, "Mr. Meland is very tired and cold and needs some sleep. Some of his clothes are also wet. Do any of you older boys have any extra clothes at school that you could loan Mr. Meland? We will wash and dry his clothes overnight above the stove."

Eldon Henning raised his hand and said, "Miss Wilson, I have a bag of clothes in my buggy in the horse barn that Mr. Meland can have. I will need to go get them. I believe it has quit snowing now, so I think I can get over there with no problem."

Miss Carrie thought for a minute. "That's a good idea. The horses need to be fed and watered, anyway. Eldon, take your brother William with you. But first, tie the three ropes in the entryway together to make one long rope. Loop one end through each of your suspenders so that you cannot be separated from one another. Then tie the other end to the flagpole. This will insure you find your way back to the school."

Within a half-hour the Henning brothers were back at the school with the clothes for the guest. The children were spreading their quilts on the floor and getting ready to bed down for the night. Carrie knew that the excitement would keep some of them awake.

Before any of them had fallen asleep Carrie announced, "Class, I would like to pray." She bowed her head and prayed, "Lord, thank You for bringing Mr. Meland safely to us. Keep him safe as he travels on, and watch over us all tonight. Be with the parents as they travel to pick up the children when the storm clears. Amen."

Early in the morning there was a great noise outside, from the horse-driven snow-removal equipment busy on the two cross-roads by the school. It was the parents of the children trying to plow away the banks of snow. Three feet of snow had fallen with drifts as high as six feet caused by the wind.

All of the children looked for Victor Meland, the man who came to them the evening before. He was gone, his clothes that had hung above the stove were gone, Eldon Henning's clothes were folded and lying on the spelling bench and the door was still locked from the inside. The children wondered how this could have happened without anyone being disturbed. Carrie knew what happened.

Carrie announced, "Children, there will be no school today. Before you go home with your parents, I want to give you a homework assignment. Write a summary of what happened yesterday and last night in our school and what you learned from the experience. Okay?"

Chapter 8

March 1915

*C*arrie's appointment was at a clinic in Moorhead on March 5th. It was the second anniversary of the shooting, and Carrie recognized and remembered it. How could she forget? Both Lewis and Jennie came with Carrie in the horse and buggy pulled by Nelly, the favorite horse of the Larson family. Lewis often said that Carrie was Nelly's favorite person. Carrie would feed her apples whenever they were available, but not too many of them.

The weather was mild with not a cloud in the sky. They took off after helping the boys with the chores. The moon was still full in the west. While he was in Moorhead, Lewis was planning to buy some seed corn for spring planting. Jennie and Carrie would do some shopping, also. They were prepared to leave Carrie overnight and return home if the doctors wanted.

On the way to the clinic Jennie asked Carrie a question. "Carrie, may I give you some motherly advice?"

"I can use all the advice I can get," Carrie replied. "Go ahead and shoot. Ah . . . bad choice of words. Go ahead and advise me."

Jennie smiled at Carrie's humorous attitude, then she took Carrie's hand and said, "Your doctor needs all of the encouragement and wisdom he can get. So I would suggest that you don't say anything that might make him worried or anxious. Don't just be a friend to him, be a *good* friend to him. This is how you can help him succeed in this delicate operation. Andrew is a choice doctor and you would be best served if he had your full support. Okay?"

"Okay, mother Jennie." Carrie answered with a smile and a loving pat on Jennie's hand.

After arriving at the clinic, Carrie began to worry. She was placed in a room all by herself waiting for a nurse and a doctor to come in. *What if the operation isn't successful?* she worried to herself. *What if Andrew refuses to operate? What if the bullet moves suddenly and damages other parts of my brain? What if Andrew cannot get to Moorhead?* Her anxious thoughts began to depress her. "This is not like me," she said out loud. "These thoughts are not of God!"

She was also worrying about her class at the Spring Prairie Township School. Was Miss Harrison a good teacher? Could she handle the Gunderson twin boys who had just moved to Spring Prairie from Canada? They were of Norwegian descent and were very hard to handle. Normally, the parents made certain that their children behaved themselves, but in these twin boys Carrie saw two troubled boys. It would be easy to say that there was not much hope in trying to correct them, but many of the parents judged the teacher by how well the children behaved. According to some parents, if a child was misbehaving it was the teacher's fault.

Then there were the costs of all of the medical procedures, including Andrew's services. He had dismissed his charges for all of his previous medical services, but what about this operation—if, indeed, it were to take place? And in light of the way Carrie had rejected his advances toward her, would he be so forgiving again? Plus, the township had already held a fundraiser at the school for the first round of hospital expenses, but many of the struggling farmers had very little in the way of discretionary funds to contribute for any future medical bills. Carrie finally decided to stop worrying and relax. After ten minutes, she laid her head against the back of the overstuffed chair and started to doze. She hadn't had much sleep the night before, and it felt good to close her eyes.

Andrew finally came into the exam room and Carrie woke up with a start. "Carrie, it's good to see you! I'm sorry to keep you waiting." He walked over to her, took her hand, and held it for a short time while he talked to her. "I never had a chance to ask you how you enjoyed the symphony concert."

Carrie and Andrew had never discussed the concert the evening of his graduation and their first official date. They were busy sharing the subject of their religious beliefs. *It was the conversation that brought into focus the difference in beliefs between us,* Carrie remembered. "Actually, I really enjoyed it. In fact, I decided to open a classical music unit within our music time at the school. I was able to borrow an RCA Victor windup phonograph and some records. The children really enjoy the music."

"Well, that's great!" Andrew responded with a broad smile. "I'm glad it was an enriching experience for you, and I'm delighted your schoolchildren have benefited from it also. I hope we can attend another concert together in the future."

"That would be fun," Carrie responded.

"Well, Carrie," Andrew said, "I understand you've been experiencing some discomfort associated with your head and back. When do you feel it?"

"When I lay my head down on a pillow I can feel a slight pain in my back and my head," Carrie answered. "I also can feel a twinge in the toes of my left foot. It's the first time I've felt anything like that since the accident . . . I've started calling it an "accident" now. Calling it a shooting brings up all kinds of questions and discussion from people . . . Occasionally, I feel the twinge in my right toes also."

"Really?" Andrew responded surprisingly. "That's interesting. Good news . . . and not unexpected. The bullet fragment is probably moving. That means it can possibly be removed."

Carrie was hoping he'd say that. "Doctor, this means that I will soon walk again."

Andrew was quiet for moment while he was listening to her breathing. Carrie was expecting a response but received none.

Andrew picked up his clipboard and wrote some things on a piece of paper. Carrie finally broke the silence. "You still don't believe me, do you Andrew?"

"Believe what?" the doctor questioned. But he knew what she meant

"My dream," answered Carrie, "or 'out-of-body experience,' as you called it."

"You mean the dream you had while you were unconscious in the hospital after your traumatic experience and surgery?" Andrew asked.

"Yes! The dream I had when you sat by the bed watching me for nearly twenty-four hours!" Carrie responded.

"Carrie, I would be a poor doctor if I practiced medicine with the use of dreams. You can dream them, interpret them, and believe them as you wish. But I need to deal with the real world . . . real data, real x-rays, real measurements, and real feelings."

"But aren't dreams real too?" Carrie asked with a certain amount of irritation.

"They are," Andrew answered, "and sometimes dreams can be wonderful, happy, and joyous. I would say that you may believe what you want and it is healthy. But can you bet the family fortune on the dream?"

"I guess you're right," Carrie responded, obviously dejected by his response. "Doctor, do you ever have dreams?"

Andrew paused for a minute and then responded in a quiet voice, "Should I tell you the truth and ask you not to tell anyone else?" he asked.

"Yes, you should," she answered.

"I have actually dreamed about you," Andrew responded with a reluctant facial expression and a hint of a blush.

"Oh really?" Carrie answered.

Andrew tried to redirect the conversation back to Carrie's situation in order to change the subject, but Carrie wouldn't let him. "What kind of a dream? Can you tell me?"

"Not now," he responded. "Maybe later."

With that the subject was changed once again to the medical condition of his patient. "What I plan to do, if you will let me, is to do an exploratory surgery where I will look to see if it's safe to remove the fragment. I have developed some new instruments and procedures for removing foreign objects from the body. If it looks right, I will proceed with the extraction."

"Thank you, Doctor," Carrie responded with relief. "You have my permission to proceed."

Andrew wanted Carrie to be at ease prior to the surgery. He knew that the part of the head where the bullet fragment was located was a difficult place to operate. He also was well aware that several other patients with the same situation died as the result of this procedure. He had performed this operation two other times. One patient made it, but one had passed on. If there were another doctor who could perform this operation, he would have had him do it. His associate in Rochester was in China for a year at this time; and since Carrie's case could not wait, it was up to Andrew.

He knew that Carrie had visited one other doctor in the past few months. Her condition was potentially critical if the bullet had somehow jarred loose. He also knew that she wanted to walk again so badly that she was willing to take any risk. But Andrew was not about to take chances in performing an operation that was risky or unnecessary. And, if during the operation the situation turned risky, he would terminate it.

Andrew did not want to embarrass Carrie, but he needed to know what any other doctors had done or said about the bullet fragment. "Tell me, Carrie, have you seen any other physicians about this bullet fragment?"

There was a noticeable pause on Carrie's part.

"I can see there's a fresh scar . . . like someone tried to work on it," Andrew pointed out.

Carrie had known she would be unable to hide the telltale sign of her impatient action, but she was still embarrassed to confess to Andrew that she was not content to wait for him to perform the surgery when the time was right. "Yes, Doctor, I consulted with one of the referrals you gave me, and the doctor from Omaha tried to operate on it. I wanted so much to walk again that I got impatient. The doctor finally told me that he did not have the technique to successfully perform this operation. He told me that there was only one doctor who could maybe perform this operation with any possibility of success." Carrie knew what Andrew's next question would be and hoped he wouldn't ask it. He did anyway.

"Did the doctor say who that doctor was?" Andrew asked.

Carrie was slow to answer. "It was you, Dr. Peterson," she answered as she choked up.

"Well, don't feel bad about it. We doctors and surgeons don't have all of the answers, although we sometimes think we do." His response made Carrie feel better.

The two of them talked for a short time longer, Andrew further explaining the procedure that he was about to perform.

"How confident are you, Doctor?" Carrie voiced in a soft tone. "Do you think that the fragment can be removed?"

Andrew needed to give Carrie some hope in what he was about to do. "I won't be completely sure until I cut into the area around the bullet fragment. By the looks of the area outside of the skin, the fragment has moved considerably. Who knows? Maybe it'll just pop out."

"I hope you're right, Doctor," Carrie replied.

Andrew took Carrie's hand and sat down on the chair next to her. "Here's the way I see it. We have only two choices: One, we can do nothing and take our chances with the bullet staying in your head for the rest of your life, . . . possibly leaving you crippled for the rest of your life, and possibly shortening your life quite considerably. Or two, we can operate, take out the fragment, and take our chances with whether you walk again. We have no guarantees."

Carrie looked intently at her doctor for a full minute, not saying a word. Carrie was having a battle in her mind about what was about to take place.

"But," Andrew said dropping Carrie's hand and folding his own hands on his lap, "I feel very confident about this surgery. And what makes me feel so confident, you might ask? I, too, dream. Last night I had a dream . . . a dream like I never have had before. "

"It sounds interesting, Doctor," Carrie responded, "Tell me about it. I love dreams. Maybe I'll add it to my book of dreams."

"I was walking by where you teach at the Spring Prairie Township School. A man dressed in farm clothes came alongside me and spoke to me."

Carrie gleamed with excitement. "What did he say?" she asked.

"He told me, 'Go ahead and operate on Miss Carrie.' Then he said to me, 'The Lord will guide your hands and give wisdom to your mind. Just remember to be patient with Carrie and take good care of her. Both of you are special with important jobs. Both of you have an important future. Together.' We continued to walk on the road and then he suddenly disappeared."

"What did he mean by 'together'?" Carrie asked.

"What do you think, Miss Carrie Wilson? There, I told you my dream.

"Thank you, Andrew. I will add it to my Book of Dreams. The book includes a chapter of the dreams of important people I know and love."

"Thank you for thinking highly enough of me that you would include my dream in your book," he said to her with a smile. Then he turned serious and said, "Carrie, I need to apologize to you for doubting you about your faith . . . and for not having enough faith myself."

Carrie leaned over and gave Andrew a hug. Now she could tell Jennie that she was nice to Dr. Andrew.

"Thank you for the hug. Sometime when we're not at the hospital or a clinic, you can give me a kiss too. But don't tell anyone," he said with a wink and a smile.

Carrie smiled back with a blush tinting her cheeks.

"We'll schedule the surgery for eight o'clock tomorrow morning," Andrew said as he concluded his appointment with Carrie. "We'll admit you to the hospital tonight, and the nurses will have you all prepped and ready to go by eight in the morning. How do you feel about having this operation?"

Carrie looked out the window as she contemplated her answer. "I trust God for what happens in my life, Andrew, and He has led me to this moment in time, with you as my doctor, and with the immediate need to get that bullet out of my body. He will prevail. That's how I feel about this operation. If it makes you feel more comfortable, I believe you are the only doctor who He wants to operate on me. I am now convinced of that. If He wants me to be crippled the rest of my life, then I will serve Him the best that I can from a wheelchair."

"Let me ask you a question, Carrie," the doctor interjected. "When this operation is completed and is successful, you will need many weeks of rehabilitation and exercise. Where will you spend that time?"

Without hesitating Carrie answered, "I plan to stay with the Larsons . . . relaxing with the family, the horses, chickens, pets, and the land."

"Good choice," Andrew responded. "Would you permit me to come and visit you? Not as a doctor, but as a good friend?"

"You may if you wish," she replied.

"I need to warn you that you may need to be in the wheelchair for a while until your leg muscles are strong enough to permit you to walk . . . if, indeed, that is the result. You may never walk like you once did, unless you have a lot of exercise."

Andrew walked out of the examination room more convinced than ever that he was in love with Carrie. He could see himself eventually spending the rest of his life with her, but he wasn't sure she could ever feel the same way. After their last meeting in Minneapolis, he was almost sure this would never happen. His colleagues had tried to convince him to accept blind dates with nurses, medical technicians, and teachers they had in mind. Adding insult to injury, they had mentioned to him on more than one occasion that he would probably be better suited with a wife who could walk. He didn't appreciate their opinions, and he let his colleagues know that.

* * * * *

Lewis and Jennie returned to the farm after they helped Carrie get admitted to the hospital. Andrew had other patients to see and he had a couple of medical classes to teach to nursing students. He decided to get a good night's sleep in preparation for the most important surgery of his career in the morning.

Carrie spent the afternoon and evening listening to the radio in the hospital lounge. She too decided that a good night's sleep was in order. She was limited to what she could eat for supper, but she really didn't have much of an appetite anyway. She had to accept the fact that she might not make it through the surgery. After all, the procedure was in the head and close to the brain. But instead of letting her fears get the better of her, she thought it would be best to write a few notes to the people close to her in case something did happen. The notes would be short and positive.

* * * * *

The next morning, Carrie was brought to the operating room and the nurses began to prepare her for surgery. As the nurses were getting ready to administer the anesthesia, Andrew walked in and asked them to wait a minute. "Carrie, I have a favor to ask of you. Would you mind praying before the operation?"

Carrie gave her doctor an amazed look. She remembered what happened the last time she prayed in a similar situation: he became embarrassed. It began a period where she and Andrew saw a spiritual division between them. She wondered what had happened since then.

"Andrew, I will pray for both of us before you operate."

Andrew seemed to be somewhat nervous. His hands were cold and slightly tense. Carrie took his two strong hands in hers, steadied them, and began to pray. "Lord, You are here with Andrew and me on this appointed day and hour. You care very much about both of us, and You have used both of us to help with a healing and hurting world and to teach many children about life and Your Word. Now we both face a big hurdle . . . even bigger than the hurdles I used to jump when I was younger.

Andrew needs to operate on my head and remove a bullet fragment that cannot stay there. Be with my doctor and once again send down an angel or two to be with us during the operation and to comfort us. Guide Andrew's hands as he operates. Give him wisdom and calm his spirit. You know that I think the world of Andrew and that You have placed him here at this time. Amen."

They both remained for a few seconds holding hands. To Carrie's surprise, Andrew continued the prayer. "Lord, be with Carrie, the nurses, and myself as we operate this morning. Help me to remove the bullet fragment. Guide my hands, and heal Carrie's body quickly. Amen."

The surgery lasted two hours. The bullet was wedged between a bone and a nerve. During the operation her body needed to remain absolutely still. Sand bags were utilized to make sure there was no involuntary movement from Carrie. Andrew had developed this particular technique specifically for Carrie's case. The doctor felt relaxed and was precise in the cuts he had to make. He felt certain that Someone was guiding his hands.

As he finished the surgery and just before he left the operating room, he took Carrie's hands in his and kissed them. There was a deep sigh from the two nurses. They knew the story.

Andrew had cleared his schedule so he could stay close by the hospital. He was also able to get away to visit Jennie and Lewis Larson on the farm twenty-four hours after the surgery, once he was sure Carrie was stable. The entire family was glad to see him. So was the horse Molly, that he had brought back from sure death after she ate too many mushrooms. Molly seemed to recognize him.

Jennie served Andrew and the Larson family a delicious lunch. When all of the dishes were done and Andrew was able to catch a few winks of sleep on the big couch, Jennie and Lewis sat down to talk to him. They both seemed nervous and didn't quite know how to start the conversation. Lewis finally said, "Doctor, Jennie and I have a question for you."

Andrew could tell his hosts were worried and said, "Yes, what would you like to know?"

"Only one question . . . will Carrie walk again?"

Andrew had expected that very question from a whole host of people, including Lewis and Jennie. The only person who could say for sure was Carrie. She was absolutely sure that she would walk again. Andrew took a deep breath and answered his hosts, "The correct answer to that question is: Only God knows."

Jennie looked at Lewis and was very surprised to hear Andrew defer to God's omniscience.

Andrew continued, "After studying Carrie's case very carefully, I have concluded that Carrie is suffering from a combination of issues that have rendered her unable to walk. Some of her problem is physical, but much more of it is of a mental nature . . . psychological."

Lewis and Jennie both leaned forward, intent on listening to every word of the doctor. Andrew took a sip of the tea that Jennie had brewed especially for him. "Continue, Doctor," Jennie said.

"Carrie endured the trauma of being shot at many times. Six bullets hit her body, any one of which could have killed her. There were two miracles that morning. One was that none of the sixteen bullets shot hit her sufficiently to kill her, and the other was that none of the children were hurt from straying lead. The killer's anger was such that he may not have cared who he killed. But maybe he did have some concern for the children. After all, the sheriff's report said that the shooter told the children to flee the building.

"However, the shooting was the last of the events that is causing the trauma. She has apparently been in fear of her attacker for quite some time. It has caused her to be slightly paranoid and not really wanting to befriend or even trust anyone who is a male.

"And there may be more. Perhaps she suffered a traumatic event in her childhood, or maybe she fears that she'll end up in a failed marriage like her parents'. I don't know what else could be contributing to the problem, and possibly even Carrie doesn't know. But this is my conclusion: I see nothing physically that should keep her from having feeling in her legs and walking."

"That's very interesting," Lewis commented. "What can be done, Doctor?"

"I'll continue to work with Carrie and be as supportive as possible. However, I may need to be firm with her to motivate her to become more forthright in overcoming some of these traumas that are quite literally crippling her."

Chapter 9

May 1915

*C*arrie remained in the hospital for the next ten days. The bullet fragment had been successfully removed, but there were some unexpected complications. The bullet had been wedged in between a bone in the neck and the nerve running to the legs. When it was removed, it caused both legs not to respond to feeling as it was hoped they would have. The nurses spent time rubbing the neck, back, and legs with only very limited and sporadic sensation reported by Carrie.

The hospital released her, providing her with crutches, a new wheelchair, and a supply of bandages to keep her healing surgical wound clean. She went to the Larson farm where she could get the love and attention she needed.

Both Carrie and Andrew were disappointed by the fact that she wasn't able to walk like Carrie had hoped. Andrew told Carrie just to be patient while the wound healed. Andrew asked Lewis if one of his daughters could help with the physical exercise. Lena volunteered and began to provide daily rubdowns and exercises to her legs.

Meanwhile, Andrew was back in the Cities providing surgery to many patients with serious bone, neck and head injuries. He was also doing some teaching at the University of Minnesota School of Medicine.

* * * * *

Around the middle of May, Andrew received a letter from Jennie stating, "Carrie is not her same old self. She is either ill or she is depressed. She seems to have something churning inside of her."

The following weekend Andrew cleared his schedule and took the train to Stockwood to see his patient. He wanted to see if he could do something for her. If nothing else, he would try to cheer her up. But there was another reason, also.

The train arrived at one in the afternoon at the Stockwood station. Andrew had no means of getting to the Larson farm as he had not let anyone at the Larson household know when he was coming. There happened to be a farmer who was about to take off on the road going north toward the country school who offered Andrew a ride. The farmer knew the Larsons and happily volunteered to take Andrew right to the farm. As they got close to where the school shooting had occurred, the farmer said, "In that school there was a terrible tragedy that occurred a while back. Some ex-boyfriend attempted to kill the teacher. It's quite a story. Maybe you read about it in the newspapers."

"I believe I did read something about it," Andrew responded. "How did it turn out?"

"Not very good for the shooter," the farmer answered, "he's now in the grave . . . the teacher is crippled."

The Larson family was glad to see Andrew once again. Carrie was in back of the house in her wheelchair getting ready to hang another load of freshly washed laundry. She did not pay attention to who was in the buggy coming up the driveway. Soon she heard the commotion and looked around to the front yard. She was surprised to see Andrew getting out of the buggy. She wasn't sure why he was at the farm—to see her or to see how she was feeling. Lena told him right away where Carrie was and Andrew walked back to the clothesline.

"Andrew?" she asked, obviously surprised to see him in Spring Prairie, "What are you doing here?"

Andrew could tell immediately that Jennie was right in her letter. Something was bothering Carrie. He could tell by her greeting. Plus, she sat somewhat slouched in her wheelchair. She just didn't seem to have the determination and spunk he was used to seeing in her.

"I wanted to see my patient, so I took the train to Stockwood," he answered. "You're still under my care, you know."

"You have a few days off, it appears, Andrew," she commented. "I was wondering when you would show up again."

Andrew looked at the two lines of clothes that Carrie had hung up earlier. "It looks like you're busy with the Larson laundry," he said as he looked at Carrie and gave her shoulder a friendly squeeze. "How do you hang the clothes up using crutches?"

"Actually," she answered, "I put two clothespins in my mouth, put the clothes item on the line, balance myself with the crutches under my arms, and use my arms and hands to pin. Like this," she said as she put her crutches in front of her and struggled to raise herself out of her wheelchair.

Andrew helped her stand from her wheelchair and said, "Carrie, you're a very innovative woman. I think you'd make a good domestic . . . maybe a good wife."

"I don't think so," Carrie answered in a dejected tone.

"Maybe we can find some time to discuss other things you have learned to do on the farm . . . and maybe some other topics." Andrew said. "But right now I'm hungry."

Jennie Larson was always prepared to serve lunch to anyone. She had a filled plate on the table within minutes. Andrew loved her cooking and hospitality, and she knew it.

"Come and have something to eat and some good coffee," she called to Andrew from an open window in the house.

Soon Andrew was eating, and Carrie was sitting across from him on the other side of the table. She never attempted to sit by Andrew. The rest of the household got the word that Andrew had arrived and were soon sitting around the table. "Thank you, Jennie. I tried to get some food in the dining car, but they had closed down. I couldn't even get a sandwich."

Andrew began thinking how he was going to get Carrie alone to speak privately with her. For some reason Carrie was in a foul mood. Andrew thought he knew the reason and he needed to talk with her about it—alone. In a flash an idea came to him. "Lewis, can I trouble you to saddle up two horses for Carrie and me to ride? I think riding will do her some good. Let's call it a new kind of therapy . . . horse therapy."

There were chuckles all around the table.

"Yes, I'll be happy to," Lewis responded. "I'll saddle up Molly and Nelly for you."

Soon Carrie and Andrew were ready to ride. Carrie was on Nelly and Andrew was on Molly. Molly again seemed to recognize Andrew from their initial encounter after the mushroom episode.

"So where are we riding off to, Andrew?" Carrie asked with a scowl on her face.

"Let's just ride to wherever. You lead the way, Carrie."

They rode along the recently flooded creek, along the newly planted corn field, and over to the Zion Lutheran Church. They stopped and Andrew lifted Carrie off her horse. Carrie could sense that Andrew was up to something. She wanted to ask him what he was doing, but she just waited for his response. He carried her into the church and set her down in a chair on the platform. It was where the pastor usually sat.

"Carrie, I don't wish to mix medicine with a personal visit, but I need to ask you how you have been feeling lately. The truth."

Carrie debated whether to tell him the truth or just sugarcoat it. "Not the best, Andrew," she admitted as tears welled up. "I so wanted to walk again . . . if that were only possible. It's supposed to happen, and I thought it would after the operation."

Andrew thought for a moment and weighed in his mind the various answers he could give to Carrie to keep her thoughts positive and give her hope. "I remember your dream, Carrie, and I was hoping it would have happened by now. I'm hopeful it still will. But I believe that there may be some other factors that are at work in your situation."

"What other factors?" she asked.

"Well, that's one of the things I wanted to talk to you about. It's why I made this trip. We'll talk about that later."

This left Carrie wondering what Andrew was talking about. She became very curious as to why Andrew was really there.

Andrew changed the subject to the pain she was still having in her back and legs. "Are you getting enough exercise and rub-downs from the Larson sisters?" he asked.

"Yes, I am," she answered.

The next place they rode the horses was over to the school across the road. Again, Andrew carried Carrie into the school. Carrie noticed that Andrew was holding her firmly against himself as he walked with her in his arms. When they were walking into the entryway, Carrie suddenly clung more tightly to Andrew. Andrew looked at Carrie's face and saw that she had closed her eyes as she passed by a spot in the entryway. He set her on the spelling bench and sat down beside her.

Andrew reached down and began to rub Carrie's ankle. "Can you feel that?" he asked.

Carrie was wondering if this was part of Andrew's medical consultation or if he was making a pass at her. She wondered how she should answer him. "Just barely, Andrew," she finally answered.

He applied more pressure to the ankle with his hands. "Can you feel any difference?" Andrew asked.

"Just slightly," Carrie responded. Now Carrie was really wondering what Andrew was up to. Andrew stood up and walked to the blackboard. He leaned against it. He noticed that Carrie's eyes shifted from his face to a spot just to his right. He looked over and saw the spot where a bullet hit from the shooters gun and had damaged the blackboard. Carrie saw him look at the blackboard and wondered where this conversation was going next.

"Carrie, I need to ask you an important question. Don't be afraid to answer it, but it is important that I hear your answer."

149

Carrie wondered what Andrew was up to now. *What possible question could he ask now that would be that important to my physical condition?* "Go ahead and ask, Andrew."

"When was the last time you kissed a man or a man has kissed you . . . passionately?"

Carrie just sat on the bench and was quiet. Of any question she thought anyone might have asked her, that would have been the least likely. She could think of only one response to Andrew's bold question.

"Andrew, why on earth could you possibly need to know the answer to that question?"

"Your answer is important." Andrew responded. He walked back to the bench and sat down. They both sat in silence for a period of time. The fact that Carrie was not answering or responding spoke volumes. He could tell she was uneasy. He finally leaned over and gave Carrie a kiss on the cheek. It surprised her but she didn't seem to mind. It was not a romantic kiss and not intended as such by Andrew. He didn't wish to make her feel any more uncomfortable than she was.

Andrew then stood up, picked up Carrie, and carried her out to the horses. They rode slowly all the way back to the Larson farm. Neither of them said a word until they arrived at the horse barn.

"Andrew, what was that all about?" Carrie asked.

Andrew dismounted Molly and stood in front of Nelly. He looked straight up at Carrie as she was sitting on her horse. He had her undivided attention. "I'm going to give it to you straight. You have survived a traumatic experience—one that very few people could have ever survived. Even people who have gone through a war with all those bullets probably would never have made it. It's a miracle that you're still breathing.

"You had five bullets removed from your body, and you were living on borrowed time with a bullet fragment still in your head, which has only just recently been removed. Even so, all of the nerves seem to be okay. *So what's the problem?* I keep asking myself."

Carrie seemed both nervous and irritated. "So what are you telling me, Doctor Andrew Peterson?" she asked cynically.

"Carrie, I think the trauma that you experienced produced a fear complex within you that you need to overcome. It is also connected to the fear you experienced with your old boyfriend. And, it's possible this fear is also caused by something that happened in your childhood or youth. I want you to think about it tonight, and we'll talk about it in the morning."

"Maybe we will," Carrie said with a hint of anger and distrust. "I cannot see where my condition has anything to do with my past. What would it be?"

"I believe you—and only you—know what it is," Andrew answered. "Think about it tonight and we'll talk tomorrow."

* * * * *

Carrie had trouble getting to sleep that night. She knew Andrew was absolutely correct in his analysis as it related to her past. She knew exactly what it was and what she had to do about it. *But how can this be accomplished without traveling back home to Massachusetts to see Mother?* she asked herself. She finally fell asleep at two in the morning.

* * * * *

It was five in the morning when Andrew woke up. Carrie had placed a blanket and a pillow on the big couch in the living room for him to sleep there. Both Lewis and Jennie were up— Lewis in the horse barn and Jennie making egg coffee, bread, and butter. Andrew waited for a cup of coffee and then decided to walk down to the creek. It was too early for Carrie to wake up, and he was worried that she may not speak to him when she did wake up. As a doctor and researcher he had several things on his mind. This visit with Carrie was priority. It concerned her future as well as his own.

The weather had been unusually violent in the past week. The Buffalo River had overflowed a few days before, which caused it to back up into all of the creeks flowing into it. The little creek that ran through the Larson property was still receding back to its original level. Consequently, it was easy to see some of the fish that had gotten caught in the many mini ponds. As the creek was going down fast, the trapped fish would soon be dead. *I wonder if Jennie has a good recipe for frying fish?* Andrew asked himself. Both Lewis and Jennie had told him about the many times they had picnics and went fishing in the Buffalo River when they worked at the mansion.

He walked back to the horse barn and found an empty five-gallon pail. He rinsed it out and then went "fishing" in the creek. His large, strong surgical hands served as the net for catching the fish. He soon had an assortment of sunfish, crappies, bass, and even four good-sized walleye. It took him only ten minutes. *This load must weigh thirty pounds,* Andrew said to himself as he was carrying it back to the farmhouse. "I don't suppose it would be very nice of me to make the Larson ladies clean fish at this time of the morning, so I guess I'll clean them myself," he said out loud.

As Andrew walked toward the door, he could see that Jennie had finished making her butter and was buttering the top of the hot bread from the oven. "Jennie, can you find me a sharp knife, a sharpening stone, and a couple of pans?" he asked as he stood just outside the kitchen door.

"What on earth are you doing, Doctor Andrew?" Jennie asked as she handed him the supplies he'd requested.

"I'm about to prepare us some fish for our breakfast, lunch, and supper. How does that sound?"

"Where did you get that many fish?" she asked, surprised at the size of his catch.

"In the Larson creek," he answered.

Carrie heard Andrew talking and was quickly wide awake at the sound of his voice. She got dressed and made it out to the kitchen using her crutches.

"Maybe Carrie will help you with cleaning them," Jennie responded as Carrie entered the kitchen. "I will also have one of the boys give you a hand. You just be careful with that sharp knife!"

Andrew laughed at the farmwife's admonishment to a skilled surgeon.

Carrie soon appeared on the porch beside Andrew. "Andrew, we were supposed to have a talk this morning, but it looks like it will need to be postponed until later."

"I think that's a good idea. Let's do it later," Andrew responded with a wink.

"How can I help you?" she asked.

Andrew was pleased that Carrie was talking to him. For some reason she sounded like she was in much brighter spirits this morning. It was like she had a change of heart toward Andrew.

Soon there was a small crew helping with cleaning fish. The Larson boys did most of the scaling while Andrew did most of the cutting of the fish. Every one of the crew spent time watching the doctor as he performed his masterful surgical artwork on the various kinds of fish. The fish were kept cold with ice from the icebox.

"You be careful with those knives, Doctor," Carrie said to Andrew. "Your hands are valuable to you, your career, and your many future patients."

She is in a good mood! Andrew concluded. *I wonder what happened last night.*

The breakfast was something that none of the Larson household had ever experienced. Fresh fish fried in butter and cornmeal, fried potatoes, Jennie's homemade brown bread, and creamed carrots comprised the menu of the morning. Because the day was very warm, the crew ate outside. Later in the morning, Theodore rode over to invite two of the neighbors to share in the lunch. They had heard about Carrie's doctor friend and wanted to meet him.

As the lunch progressed Andrew kept looking at Carrie. He had never watched her like this since she was unconscious in the hospital after the shooting. Carrie noticed Andrew smiling at her and she even broke into a big smile back at him. What was going on?

It had been such a happy morning and everyone was in good spirits. The temperature was getting hotter by the minute, and the air was sultry and sticky for everyone. This day would bring other excitement.

When the lunch dishes had been cleared and its participants had been dispersed back to their chores, it was time for Andrew to prepare to return to his job in the Cities. He would board the train later that afternoon, but first he needed to talk to Carrie. He needed to convince her to deal with the mental block that he thought was keeping her from walking. He was also in love with her, and it was his desire to marry her. The problem was that she was not in love with him—at least, she wasn't showing it. These two issues were separate but related. Unless she would deal with the first issue, the second one could never happen.

Andrew asked Carrie to accompany him to the mailbox where they both needed to mail a letter. He pushed the wheelchair while they talked. When they arrived at the end of the long driveway, he turned the wheelchair around so that she was facing him. Then he sat down on the big flat rock and thought about how to put into words what he wanted to say.

"Carrie, do you have any desire to marry me?" Andrew asked bluntly.

Carrie was not surprised by his question—only by the way he asked it. "I figured you would ask me that question . . . soon."

"So what's your answer?" Andrew responded. "In fact, let me rephrase the question. Carrie, will you marry me?"

Carrie sat quietly for a moment. She had been expecting Andrew's proposal for months and had thought about what she would say when the time came. "Andrew, I need some time before I can give you an answer. I have been so resistant to having any feelings whatsoever for any man, that I don't honestly know how I truly feel about you. I know you are in love with me, but I need to make sure I can make the same commitment to you. Could I ever let myself fall in love with you? In my current mental condition, probably not. But I want to give you some good news. After talking to you yesterday, I now know the unresolved issue in my past that is maybe blocking my full recovery. I wrote my mother a letter last night and poured out my heart to her. It's a start, but I will need to talk to her in person before the issue can be fully resolved."

"I can't wait forever, Carrie."

"I know, Andrew, and I wouldn't expect you to. That wouldn't be fair to you. But I can't help thinking that maybe you need someone who will be more of an aid to your profession. Also, if your place of employment is the city, what would I do in a city? And my heart is in teaching. If I get married, social protocol dictates that I need to quit my job and start having babies. I'm not sure I'm ready to do that."

"Why couldn't we attempt to be happy just being married to each other no matter where we live or what we do?" Andrew responded. "How long would it take for you to fall in love with me?"

Carrie didn't know how to answer Andrew's question. "Come over to me," Carrie beckoned with outstretched arms.

Andrew walked over to Carrie's wheelchair. She took his hands in hers, then she pulled him toward her, reached up, and gave him a passionate kiss.

"You're back, Carrie," Andrew said with a sigh of relief.

"I know . . . and I feel wonderful," she answered.

As they embraced each other and enjoyed the comfort of each other's company, Andrew noticed the weather was getting more sultry and hotter by the minute. He recognized the atmosphere as being exactly the same as the day a tornado hit in his township home in Iowa when he was a teenager. *We're going to get something out of this,* he thought to himself.

* * * * *

The three younger Larson children were on a picnic down by the creek when the storm clouds started gathering in the west. The children—Joe, Roy, and Louise—had brought with them paper tablets with which they would make paper boats and sail them on the part of the creek where the water formed a pond. It was only when the creek flooded that it formed such a place for the children to swim or sail boats. They had packed a picnic and headed out along the creek to their favorite spot just after the noon lunch. Sometimes all three of them would ride one of the horses to this spot, but this time they were on foot.

About three in the afternoon, the sky in the west began to get very dark. There was a wide stretch of almost black clouds starting just above the horizon and extending up about thirty degrees. Above and in front of this bank of clouds was another churning gray-colored mass of clouds. Everyone except the three picnicking children was on the Larson farm lawn watching the colorful atmospheric display in the northwest.

Lewis and Jennie were becoming very worried for their three missing children. Both of them were having the same thoughts. They did not wish to lose any more children like they did in 1901, and these children sailing boats had the same names. News had already reached Spring Prairie that the day before tornados were reported in both North Dakota and South Dakota. Farms had been destroyed with some lives being lost and scores of injuries. Also, the day before it had hailed in the Spring Prairie Township, some of it the size of baseballs. Jennie had gathered up a few bucketsful and placed them in the cool basement icebox.

Andrew made the decision to wait until the next morning to return to St. Paul and to his work. He wanted to talk further with Carrie about the future.

Andrew looked at Lewis and Jennie and saw the worry on their faces. He decided to do something to ease their concern in a hurry. He did not think they realized the magnitude of the impending storm or the danger the children were in. "Lewis," he said in an urgent tone of voice, "let's you and me run and get the children. Now. This storm is coming up very fast. I have a very good friend in Minneapolis who has studied meteorology at the university, and he has told me of the warning signs and dangers of these storms. Those signs are in the sky and atmosphere right now, and they're nothing to fool with. All of the rest of you stay here and get yourselves protected in the basement shelter . . . the southwest corner. You may want to let some of the livestock out of the buildings before you go in, just in case the buildings are hit."

Carrie was intently watching and listening to the person who had just proposed to her. The letter she had written to her mother had already started to have its effect on her mental state, and she had a peace of mind she hadn't experienced since childhood.

Andrew and Lewis did not wait. They took off running around the machinery and onto the path to the creek, jumping over tree logs and around piles of gathered rocks from the fields. Lewis knew about where the children were playing. It had to be close to where Andrew had caught the fish only hours before. The creek was still receding from the recent flood; but if there were rain with the coming storm, it would be filling up again.

Meanwhile, the entire household was gathered on the front porch waiting to descend into the cellar, including Carrie who was ready to negotiate the difficult wooden stairway with the aid of her crutches. Most everyone was frantic and scared. Freddie and Theodore ran to the barn and let some of the livestock out.

Meanwhile, Andrew was outpacing Lewis as he ran along the shore of the creek. Lewis had told him where the children would be playing. "Just follow the creek to where the water has gathered into a large pond. The children will be somewhere on the shore. The children have never seen a tornado and have no idea of the dangers involved." Lewis tried his best to keep up with Andrew.

Andrew's still youthful legs and physically fit body enabled him to move as fast as the uneven terrain permitted. He was soon at the creek. He kept his eyes both on the creek shoreline ahead of him and on the line of black clouds to the northwest. A funnel cloud emerged out of a big gray cloud and started lowering itself down to the ground, swaying like an elephant's trunk. The tornado appeared to be headed toward the pond where the children were. Andrew took a quick look back to see where Lewis was—not far behind.

Andrew tried desperately to formulate a plan for how to protect the children, Lewis, and himself from the violent weather headed their way. *They won't be able to outrun the funnel,* he said to himself, *it's too close. If we lie on the ground we could be pummeled by flying and rotating debris. Even worse, we could be caught up into the funnel and carried many miles . . . even killed in midair by the rotating debris.* Andrew sent up a plea to God to show him the way.

* * * * *

In the Larson cellar Carrie said in a shaky voice, "I'm going to pray for God's protection, if you don't mind."

"Please do, Carrie," Jennie replied.

"Lord, I need to ask You to protect the children, Lewis, and Andrew from this coming storm. Help Lewis and Andrew find the children quickly and get them back home to us. Give all of us calm and peace. Amen."

* * * * *

Andrew soon saw the children and yelled to them, "Louise, Joe, Roy . . . let's go!" They quickly responded and ran toward him and their dad, who by this time had caught up with the young doctor.

"There's a storm coming," Roy yelled out sounding frightened, "we're going to get wet!"

As the children were running toward them, Andrew looked up and saw that the tornado was on the ground and growing in size and intensity, moving its tail back and forth. *What do I do now, God?* he prayed. He frantically looked for a shelter and noticed where the creek flowed under the roadway only about one hundred feet away. There was an iron culvert about three feet in diameter running under the road. It was only half filled with water. A peaceful voice from somewhere deep inside of him seemed to tell him, *Hide in there and you'll be safe.*

"Come this way, children," Andrew yelled over the noise of the oncoming funnel cloud, "Quickly." He grabbed little Louise around her stomach with one arm and grabbed Roy's hand with the other arm, and ran toward the culvert opening. Lewis picked up Joe and followed Andrew. They waded quickly into the water and to the culvert.

Andrew gently guided Louise's head into the culvert opening and then quickly followed her in. Roy and Joe followed with Lewis carefully pushing them in. Their father was the last one in. The five of them were now in eighteen inches of water. "Okay, kids, grab onto each other and hang on for dear life with all the strength you have. Keep your heads above the water and close your eyes and mouth. Lewis, try to keep the children from being sucked out of the culvert. Everybody . . . hang onto each other." Andrew had to shout very loud to compete with the noise and vibration from the twister.

The noise outside was earsplitting. It sounded like several freight trains traveling all at once on top of them. The vibration shook the ground. Little Louise was starting to cry. "Be brave, Louise," Andrew yelled out over the loud atmospheric clamor and ground rumble.

There was a pull from each end of the culvert. The water flowing through the culvert all drained out from the twister's air pressure suction. Andrew had his one hand holding Louise's ankle, his other hand onto Joe's belt, and his legs wrapped around Roy's waist. Lewis was holding Louise around the waist with one arm and had hold of Joe's arm with his other hand. The five of them were hanging onto each other and were inseparable. The maximum pull lasted for a full minute, then it slowly died down. They waited in silence for two additional minutes. The water began to slowly refill the culvert.

"Okay, Lewis, move back out to the opening," Andrew said in a quieter, calmer voice. Soon they were all out. The funnel had sucked much of the water out of the mini lake. They all waded through the mud and muck.

"Look good at that cloud, children. You will be telling your own children and grandchildren about it someday," Lewis said almost reverently.

Andrew watched the funnel cloud for a minute or so and noticed it was moving toward a farmhouse about a mile away.

He knew it was going to hit the farm. "I wonder if those farmers are in their cellar . . . or if they even have a cellar."

"That's the Sneller farm, and they don't have a cellar," Lewis said, "I helped them build that house and barn."

"Children, run home with your dad. I'm going to stay and watch this funnel cloud to see if it hits their house and barn."

As Andrew expected, the funnel took a small building on the edge of the farm. Then it moved toward the barn and house, taking the roofs and the contents. "Those poor people," he said out loud.

Lewis and his children raced back to the Larson farmhouse. One by one they arrived—first Roy, then Joe, then Louise, and finally Lewis. They were covered with mud and were soaking wet. Andrew was missing from the group and Carrie's heart sank. "Where is Andrew?" she asked.

"He stayed to watch where the tornado went next," Lewis answered, "He'll soon be here."

The children were tripping over each other's words telling what had just happened to them—how they hid in the culvert. Within five minutes Andrew, wet and looking terrible, sprinted up to the house.

"You have saved our children's lives," Jennie cried as she gave her husband and Andrew each a hug. Carrie came over to Andrew and gave him an embrace and long hug.

Andrew said with great urgency, "I need to be taken over to the farm just southeast of your place. The tornado has hit their farmhouse, the barn, and machine shed. I stood and watched the twister demolish the entire farm. If there were people in that twister, there have to be some injuries. Can one of you boys get me a horse and buggy? I need to take my medical bag with. Carrie, you can come along with to help. Lewis, can you take the wagon over in case anyone is seriously injured? They may need to be taken to a hospital. Maybe Jennie and the girls could bring some water and blankets."

Andrew lifted Carrie onto the horse-drawn buggy. He also placed her crutches into the buggy. They drove over to the Sneller farm just southeast of the Larson farm. As they got closer, there was nothing but destruction as far as the eye could see. Even the windmill was in a mass of twisted steel.

They drove up the driveway, having to steer the horse and carriage around broken tree limbs, shredded lumber, and mangled machinery. Many of the animals were lying on the ground, either dead or in the process of dying. Carrie put her hand on Andrew's arm and said, "What's that? . . . It sounds like a couple of children crying. I recognize their cry."

They stopped where a part of an upstairs had been carried away by the funnel. Andrew jumped off of the buggy and carefully pulled off the pieces of lumber where the Sneller children's cries were coming from. One by one he handed the boy and the girl to Carrie sitting in the buggy, placing one on either side of her. She carefully hugged them in case either of them had any injuries. They quickly stopped crying in Carrie's comforting arms.

Andrew walked toward the demolished barn and listened for any other signs of life. There were two of them—one from within a pile of rubble and another one from against the steel frame of the windmill that had been torn out of its cement foundation. He quickly ran to the windmill sound. There was a woman with her arm having a compound fracture, among other cuts and bruises. She was losing blood fast. He took off his shirt and made a tourniquet and applied it to her arm. She was unable to walk, so he gently carried her over to where Carrie was sitting with the two children in the buggy and placed Mrs. Sneller by her children.

He next ran to where the other sound in the rubble had been heard. "This has to be what's left of the barn," he said out loud. Frantically tearing at the rubble, he brought out Mr. Sneller covered with dirt, mud, and blood. He carried the man over to where the rest of his family was resting. Except for the woman's loss of blood and broken arm, everyone seemed to be relatively okay and their lives were not in any danger.

While all of this activity was going on, Carrie was carefully watching her doctor, Andrew. She was well aware that she was still to give him a definite answer to his proposal for marriage. One question kept nagging at her: *Why would Andrew want to marry a cripple? Why would Andrew want to marry a woman who would be a burden to him? . . . I guess he has his reasons,* she said to herself. But as she watched him move in the midst of tragedy, she realized that he was not just a skillful doctor, he really cared about people. *And he cares for me,* she realized.

Carrie knew the time for decision was now, and she made up her mind. She realized that she was truly and genuinely in love with Andrew, but her irrational fear about men had kept her from admitting and accepting it. She would enthusiastically accept Andrew's proposal. It remained a question of when to tell him. Now was not the time. They had more important things on their minds

Meanwhile, the Larson family was on their way over to the neighbor's devastated farm. They brought on the wagon some sheets, water, food, and blankets. As they approached the farm they did not recognize any of the buildings until they saw the familiar well with the spring water. The spring water was used back in 1901 during the diphtheria epidemic.

They saw the family sitting in the buggy with Andrew and Carrie. Andrew was giving first aid to the two children and their parents. As it was still hot even after the tornado had gone, everyone was thirsty. Jennie made sure everyone had a good drink of water. "Thank you, Jennie . . . and my family thanks you," Mr. Sneller said.

"It looks like all four of them sustained some injuries," Andrew said, "so I think we should take them to the doctor in Glyndon. The mother has a bad cut on the arm where the broken bone pierced the skin and needs stitches. She also has a possible broken leg. I don't have the materials to set her leg or the arm. The dad and the two children look like they fared a little better, but they need to be checked over also. Carrie and I can take them in the wagon into Glyndon right away. The mother needs blood fast."

Soon Carrie and the doctor were on their way to Glyndon with the injured family. On the way they were stopped twice to pick up two more injured persons at other farms. The doctor saw where the tornado had meandered through the countryside leaving in its wake a wide path devastation and mayhem.

When they got to Glyndon, the doctor's office was closed. Andrew then decided to go on to the Northwestern Hospital in Moorhead. "I fully understand why they closed the office," Andrew said, "The doctor is most certainly making farm calls."

Once the patients were admitted into the hospital, Andrew and Carrie decided it was too late to travel back to the Larson farm. "We'll need to stay in town overnight here at the hospital. There are two guest rooms available. I'll get some fresh bedding, towels, and gowns for us."

Andrew spent a considerable amount of time getting cleaned up from the muddy experience in the culvert. He was able to get a clean set of clothes from the hospital laundry room. Carrie also cleaned up after an active day and checked into the room next to Andrew's.

* * * * *

At the Larson farm, the telegraph operator from the Stockwood train depot delivered a message to Lewis and Jennie by horseback. Andrew had sent a wire that he and Carrie would be spending the night in Moorhead and would return in the morning. All of the telephone lines were down, so a telegraph message was the only communication method available.

"I'm glad he let us know that," Lewis said to Jennie, "I was getting worried about them. What a day! I still cannot believe how dirty the children and I were. Not only were we wet, we were muddy and stinky from the creek water and mud. There was a sticky muck on the inside of that culvert. I have never appreciated being clean and dry as much as I do now!"

* * * * *

Over dinner at the Nightingale Café Andrew said to Carrie, "Thank you for your help today, Carrie. You did a good job."

"I really didn't do that much," she replied.

"Ah, but you did," Andrew replied. "You kept the two little ones quiet while I gave attention to their parents. And you kept me focused by thinking about you."

"What do you mean, Andrew?" Carrie asked.

"Well, I'm still waiting for an answer to my proposal to you."

"Well," Carrie answered, "I have an answer for you. I will marry you for one reason. I am in love with you. I can't stop thinking about you. I want to be with you."

Andrew grabbed Carrie sitting next to him and gave her a big, long kiss. "And I love you too, Carrie. We'll always remember this day . . . for more than one reason. We survived a devastating tornado, and you accepted my marriage proposal.

Later that evening, they were sitting in the doctors' lounge. Andrew had contacted his office in St. Paul and told them that he would not be returning for a couple of days.

Carrie and Andrew were holding hands when she decided to ask her doctor and future husband a question. "Where and when should we have a wedding?"

"I'm going to let you decide the answers to those questions," the doctor answered. "Whatever you decide is fine with me. I couldn't be happier that you've agreed to spend the rest of your life with me. Whatever you want, you may have."

Carrie asked the doctor another question. "Do you think I can walk down the aisle using my crutches?"

"We have enough time that maybe you'll be able walk without your crutches," he answered.

"Do you really think so, Andrew?" Carrie asked with excitement in her voice.

"I believe the chances are very good," Andrew said, "I believe God will cause it to happen, and I think something is going to happen that will bring it about."

"I think I know what's keeping me from walking. It's my mother. I have never forgiven her for what she did to me when I was a little girl."

"What did she do?"

Carrie answered, "She slapped me twice . . . across the mouth . . . in front of my friends. I need to take care of that and forgive my mom, but I need to talk to her in person. I sent her a letter this morning. That small step has started the ball rolling . . . at least on my part."

* * * * *

After a good night's sleep in the guest rooms, Andrew and Carrie left early for Spring Prairie. They left at first light—shortly after four in the morning—and arrived at the Larson farm by six. Everyone was just sitting down at the breakfast table. As they entered the kitchen, there was a burst of applause. Everyone wanted to know about the Sneller family. Both Andrew and Carrie shared some reports that they had seen along the road and stories that they had heard at the hospital from other victims of the tornado.

After the table grace was said by little Louise, Lewis announced the work to be done for the day. "The work today is threefold. First, we need to go back to the Sneller farm and help organize the cleanup for them. My guess is other neighbors will be there and wanting to help out. Second, one of us needs to take Doctor Andrew to the Stockwood depot so he doesn't miss his train. And finally, we have hay to put up into the barn, once it's dry. It doesn't sound like much fun, but it's got to be done."

Carrie interrupted Lewis and said, "I have something to say." Everyone wondered what it was, although they all had an idea of what it could be. The family was very close knit, and it was most difficult to keep a secret from anyone. Jennie and Lewis were very much aware of Carrie and Andrew's feelings for one another. "Andrew has made a marriage proposal to me and I have accepted."

Everyone stood and cheered as Andrew grabbed Carrie and gave her a passionate hug and kiss. The breakfast quickly turned into a celebration. Lewis and Jennie each wondered what may be in store for the couple with Carrie's handicap.

Chapter 10

August 1915

On the first of August Carrie was busy planning for the wedding. It was also a period of exercise and healing in anticipation of her attempting to walk again. No one was completely sure that she would—or even could—walk again. Not even Carrie herself. The hope of her walking again was the fact that she was once again having increased feeling in both legs. Andrew was convinced that nothing was physically wrong with Carrie. There had to be something going on mentally that was keeping her from freely moving her legs. Andrew was no psychological therapist; but after being her doctor for over two years, he was convinced that the problem was not purely physical. Carrie knew what the problem was and had taken the first step to remedy it—asking her mother to forgive her.

The fragment of the bullet had been saved by Andrew at the request of Carrie. What she intended to do with it was not revealed by her. She apparently was going to make something out of it. Just the fact that she wanted to keep the lead fragment was an indication that she was past the shooting tragedy.

The doctor had Carrie on a rigid exercise program. She moved her legs both by herself and with one of the Larson girls assisting her. Because of the many months in the wheelchair and from using crutches, Carrie's back was beginning to feel some strain. The doctor had prescribed a series of exercises to alleviate that problem, and Carrie was relieved they seemed to be helping. He had also prescribed a medicine to relax her at night so she could get some rest.

Carrie and Andrew had talked about when and where they should get married. The Zion Lutheran Church was one possibility. There was plenty of room for the guests and the reception. However, Andrew thought that maybe having it at the church would raise unneeded discussion and questions about the tragic school shooting incident just across the road.

It was suggested by Jennie and Lewis that the wedding be held at the Larson farm. In case of rain, a recently constructed and not-yet-in-use machine shed could be used for the ceremony, and the house would have to do for the reception. A couple of tents would be used to handle any overflow from the house or if the weather was too hot.

Concerning the date for the wedding, Andrew had to be at his work in a St. Paul hospital on September 1. Carrie had already resigned from her teaching position at the Spring Prairie Township School and would find a teaching job close to where they would be living in St. Paul.

Carrie wished to have her family come from Massachusetts to attend the wedding. Having her separated parents attend the wedding was somewhat worrisome for Carrie. Where would they stay? Should she suggest a hotel in Moorhead or Hawley? Carrie finally decided this detail could be worked out by her parents. Many of the neighbors had offered to help with other details of the wedding.

A date of August 21st was decided on by Andrew and Carrie for the noon wedding. They chose to have the wedding ceremony on the south and east sides of the front yard of the Larson farm next to the young cottonwood trees that Lewis had planted years before. The reception would be held on the west side of the house.

The food would be a Scandinavian smorgasbord comprised of both Norwegian and Swedish delicacies. The only item that was not included on the list was lutefisk. Lewis, being Norwegian, loved the ethnic dish. His wife, being Swedish, could not get past the smell. Jennie having 13 babies in her lifetime viewed eating or even smelling lutefisk as something she called "ishda."

Andrew had a few days off from his appointments at the Moorhead clinic and decided to take Carrie on an afternoon date. He wanted to see some of the county that Lewis and Jennie Larson had often talked about. He asked Lewis if they could borrow one of the horses and a buggy. The answer was yes, of course. Jennie packed a picnic lunch for the doctor and Carrie and they took off at about noon.

"Where are we going Andrew?" Carrie asked.

"Where do you want to go?" Andrew answered.

"Let's go the Buffalo River Mansion," Carrie answered.

Soon Andrew was driving Molly and the buggy toward the mansion where Lewis and Jenny had first met and often talked about. Carrie had been given a tour from Jennie soon after she first began teaching at the Spring Prairie school. Her main interest was some legend that Jennie had talked about only once, but that tickled Carrie's curiosity.

"Andrew," she said as they were on their way to the mansion, "let's see if we can find the Indian graveyard."

"What Indian graveyard?" Andrew responded.

"Jennie has mentioned it to me only once," Carrie answered.

"Sure," Andrew answered. "What is it and where is it?"

"Jennie told me about a legend that has been rumored but not verified. It's an Indian graveyard that is a short distance from the mansion . . . across the river. Let's see if we can find it." Carrie was thinking that there would probably be a pathway and bridge for her wheelchair.

Andrew went inside the mansion and asked if they knew where the Indian graveyard was. Nothing was known, other than the rumor that was at various times spread about. Andrew figured that it had to be on the other side of the Buffalo River, probably hidden in the woods. "This is not going to be easy, Carrie," he said. "Our first task is to get to the other side of the river. The river is still quite high from the recent rains. They did tell me inside the mansion that there is no bridge to walk across. I may have to carry you across, if we can find a place in the river that is not too deep. Maybe we can find a fallen tree along the river."

Andrew was halfway hoping Carrie would finally say to skip the adventure to find the graveyard and suggest some other place to visit. There was a long pause as he sat in the buggy waiting for Carrie's response.

Andrew assumed Carrie had a great interest in Indian history and culture. When she taught at the Amish school in Pennsylvania, she studied what history was known about an Indian people close to the colony. She had become fascinated with the culture of that particular group of Americans.

Finally, Carrie voiced the challenge for Andrew. "Do you think you can carry me across the river?"

Andrew took Carrie's hand and said, "I believe I can carry Carrie across the Buffalo River."

She smiled at Andrew's attempt at humor.

"But first let's see if we can find a fallen tree that extends all the way across the river," Andrew continued.

They tied the horse and buggy to a tree and started to walk east on the bank along the north side of the river. There was a path that the guests of the mansion had used and worn down over the years. Carrie and Andrew followed the path as it led around trees, bushes, and big rocks. Carrie was walking ahead of Andrew using her crutches. It was slow going at first, but she soon learned to make the twists and turns with great ease. He watched very closely in case she fell. They walked for twenty minutes on the path that followed close to the river.

Andrew suddenly stopped and called out to Carrie, "I see a fallen tree!"

"Where?" Carrie asked.

"Up ahead . . . where the river narrows all of a sudden. It looks like a huge tree that has fallen recently . . . maybe during the rains and flood, or during the tornado. The massive cottonwood tree is at least four feet in diameter. I'll have to carry you on the tree across the river," Andrew said.

"Let me try walking across on crutches," Carrie suggested.

"Okay. But be careful. I'll follow right behind you and be ready to catch you," Andrew said.

Just getting on the tree was a major task. Andrew lifted her up and laid her flat on her back. Then he got onto the tree himself. Getting Carrie upright again was not an easy task; but he managed to lift her up, holding her steady until she felt balanced.

Andrew was amazed at how skillfully Carrie navigated the huge fallen tree across the river. Only once did she falter when a large fish suddenly jumped out of the water and startled her. Andrew quickly grabbed her around the stomach. Carrie hung onto her crutches. Andrew hugged his future wife close to him. "You may let go now," Carrie announced. "I have my balance once more."

"Let me hang on some more," Andrew said longingly.

"We can do that later," she responded, "I don't want us both to fall in to the river and get wet or maybe drown."

"That headline would be a good one," Andrew said. "Miracle teacher drowns in Buffalo River."

They both laughed and finally Andrew let go of her.

Once they were on the other side of the river, they began the search for the graveyard. Andrew had no idea what they were looking for other than a group of large stones that may resemble gravestones or a mound of earth. Carrie had a little trouble walking with crutches through the tall summer prairie grass. A couple of times Andrew had to carry Carrie across a small ravine or over a mound.

At one spot they came close to a herd of cattle that were grazing. The animals paid no attention to the couple, even when Andrew asked one of the cows, "Where are the Indian burial sites?" The cow never answered.

They soon came upon a group of large trees between which someone had seemingly carefully placed rocks, about two to three feet in diameter. It was like the trees were purposely planted between the rocks. Upon close examination, a faint color of paint could be seen—like it had been applied fifty to a hundred years in the past. "Is this really an Indian graveyard?" Carrie asked.

"It's possible," Andrew answered. "One would need to study the history of the Indians living around this area of Minnesota, if it is known. Also, one would need to know the burial customs of these people." After a few moments Andrew added, "Maybe we could make that a nighttime hobby after we get married."

"I don't think so," Carrie said doubtfully.

The walk back to the mansion side of the river was not without a spill off of the tree crossing the river. Fortunately, Andrew was a good swimmer and was able to catch Carrie only one foot below the water line. Both of them were soaked with water.

"Now what are we going to do?" Carrie asked.

Andrew offered a solution. "Let's walk back to the buggy, undress except for our underclothes, hang the wet clothes on the front and rear of the buggy, and then drive the buggy back toward Spring Prairie. The park is practically empty, so no one will see us. You can wear my shirt, just in case. On the way back to the farm, the wet clothes will dry. We can put the clothes on before we arrive home."

"Sounds good to me," Carrie replied.

As they passed through the railway underpass, they both noticed that some of the people standing along the track next to the stopped passenger train were looking at what they saw inside the buggy. The women quickly looked away, but some of the men stood staring with mouths agape.

"Andrew, I love your undershorts," Carrie whispered in his ear with a giggle.

As they were making the trip back to the Larson farm, they continued their discussion of what they thought their life would look like in a few years. Their discussion disregarded the fact that Carry had a handicap that may have an occasional effect on some of their activities. They both agreed that each could live with whatever came their way, as long as they loved each other.

* * * * *

The morning of their wedding day, both of them were up by six in the morning. This was the day both of them had been waiting for. They both knew that the expected crowd of guests had been anticipating this wedding also, as it would be different from what they were accustomed to. Besides the fact that the bride would be either rolled down the aisle using a wheelchair, or would walk using a pair of crutches, a doctor was marrying his patient. Then there was the miracle story of the bride surviving a sixteen-bullet murder attempt, the report of which had been spread all over the country by the news stories. Added to it was a groom who went through a tornado inside a culvert with a farmer and three children. Everyone was excited to witness the "happily ever after" moment for these two incredible individuals.

An hour before the wedding started, Carrie's parents arrived in their rented carriage. Carrie wheeled herself to the driveway to greet them. She and her mother Molly had been exchanging letters for the past month in preparation for the wedding. They now seemed to be communicating on an agreeable level. There was only one thing that they both needed to do. Carrie needed to initiate the action and it had to be done in private. They both knew what it was, as Carrie had written to her mother a month previous.

As they met, the tears began to flow from both of them. Mother and daughter hugged each other warmly and Molly kissed Carrie on the cheek. "Carrie, can you forgive me for being such a prudish and mean mother?" she appealed to her daughter.

Carrie was surprised at what she had just heard her mother ask. She had planned to begin the conversation, but her mother beat her to it. "Yes, of course I will," Carrie answered. "And now will you forgive me for being bitter for what happened when I was a little girl? I vowed to myself back then that I would never forgive you for slapping me in front of my Italian rope-jumping friends. Remember?"

"I do remember, but I have forgotten about that, Carrie."

"Well, I didn't forget about it, and I have stored up a bitter feeling through the years just thinking about it. I have harbored that negative feeling against you for all of these years. Bitterness is a negative thought watered by time. Now I'm asking you to forgive me."

"I will and I do," Molly said. "Oh, Carrie . . . I'm so proud of you." There was a private period of embracing and tears behind the carriage. Oleg had ridden in the same carriage from Moorhead. He stood by and was pleasantly surprised at what he was witnessing. Carrie hoped that maybe now there may be an answer to her prayers for her parents reconciling with each other.

The guests arrived at the Larson farm from many places. Some of the people came directly from the railroad stations in Stockwood and Glyndon. Many came in horse-drawn buggies from the countryside. Some, living close by on farms, came on foot since it was a nice day with not a cloud in the sky. Some even came in automobiles that they had purchased recently and had learned to drive.

All of Miss Wilson's students were there with their parents. They were all sitting together.

All of the chairs had been hauled by wagon from the church, along with much of the dinnerware. Everyone found a good place to sit with many sitting on the green grass. The lawn had been mowed by the Larson boys using the push mower. The flower beds were cleaned of any weeds. Quite noticeable was the small gravestone garden off to the northeast of the house: the graves that contained the bodies of the three Larson children who had died in the summer of 1901. That was a very unhappy time. By contrast, this day would be a very happy day for two people and their guests.

The big moment arrived and Carrie was all set to be wheeled down the long white sheet stretching from the back door to the front yard. Everyone was in place. Oleg Wilson was standing at the beginning of the white runner, ready to push his daughter Carrie's wheelchair down the aisle.

Out of nowhere there emerged a large pregnant sow that a neighbor had dropped off at the Larson farm that morning. There were a few giggles, some gasps, and a few faces of unbelief. The hog had just walked from an open gate leading out of the hog pen and onto the white sheet. The hog, Bertha, had been a pet of the neighbor's children and was comfortable around people.

Neither Andrew nor Carrie were very pleased and thought it would ruin their wedding. Three of the younger Larson children—Roy, Louise, and Joe—had fed the hog while visiting the neighbors and knew what to do. Louise and Joe ran to the table where the wedding food was being placed. They each grabbed a couple pieces of pickled herring and ran to where the hog had stopped. Bertha did not know where to go next. She just stared at all of the guests.

The children placed their hands containing the pickled herring on Bertha's snout. The hog smelled the herring and started to back away from the children. When Bertha had backed to within about ten feet of where Carrie was in her wheelchair, she suddenly turned around and ran right into the side of the wheelchair. Carrie was thrown from the chair and was on the ground lying on the white sheet. There was a chorus of gasps from the crowd. Without thinking, Carrie did what she was used to doing since she began using the wheelchair—she used her arms and pushed herself up off the ground. She was soon standing on her feet and reaching for the wheelchair Oleg had set upright for her. Then she stood without her hands on the chair for support. It was the first time since the tragic shooting she had stood on her own without the use of her crutches.

Andrew started to run toward Carrie when he saw she had tipped over, but halfway to her he stopped when he saw her standing.

Carrie looked down along the white sheet soiled with dirt and mud that Bertha had tracked across it. She was at a moment of decision. God was telling her to walk down the aisle and stand next to her husband-to-be. She knew she could make it. It was where God's miracle in her life would be continued—where her dream in the hospital and the present met. It was Carrie's destiny.

She took Oleg's arm and started out walking very unsteadily, praying with every step that she would not fall. So did the breath-holding audience. Andrew started walking toward her again to help her. "No, Andrew . . . I can make it to you," Carrie called to him in a confident voice, which all of the silent guests heard.

Everyone was absolutely still and awestruck. No one said a word, and some didn't even dare to breathe. They were witnessing a miracle right in front of their eyes. Only Carrie was not surprised. Nobody else could believe it.

Andrew wanted to run down the aisle way and grab her—maybe even carry her the rest of the way. Carrie was determined to go it by herself. As she continued, her steps became easier. As she got to within a few steps of the pastor and Andrew, her school students sitting on the grass began to applaud. It started a prolonged applause. The wheelchair was moved away from the crowd and parked by the house—never again to be used by Carrie.

The rest of the wedding went off without a hitch with many of the guests either praying or sobbing for happiness. For the recessional, Andrew proudly escorted his wife back up the soiled silk sheet. People had been so used to helping Carrie with her handicap that watching her walk under her own power seemed unreal. But Carrie had prepared herself for this moment in time, and she rejoiced its timely arrival.

* * * * *

Andrew and Carrie had planned to spend the first night of their honeymoon at the Buffalo River Mansion. The owners made sure that the best room was available for them. Jennie Larson had contacted her former employer and did some planning without Andrew and Carrie knowing. There was to be a special banquet in their honor and a dance in the Blue Room.

For the first time since the accident, Carrie was able to dance. She and Andrew were good dancers and everyone had a good time.

After the dance and prior to the bride and groom retiring for the night, they went for a midnight swim. It was the first time Carrie had been swimming since the shooting. Her legs were still a little weak from lack of use, so Andrew had to help her so she would not to fall as she entered the water. But soon she was swimming almost as well as Andrew.

The next morning they had a long talk about the future. "Carrie, I want you to have the life of your choosing . . . to have a career, at least until our children come along, or to just be my wife. What do you want to do?"

Carrie thought a while trying to decide how she should respond to him. She had thought often about the future. "Here's what I would like to have us do. Your career is priority and will provide us with a good income. But I would like to do more teaching. So being we are going to live in Minneapolis, I will find a job teaching at one of the elementary schools until I become pregnant. Then I will stay at home and put my full effort into taking care of our children. When the children leave home, I will go back to teaching school."

"And we will thank God every day for the miracle He has performed in Carrie Peterson's life," Andrew added.

"And Dr. Andrew Peterson will continue to do the work of helping God's healing and suffering people," replied Carrie.

The End